I0587384

FROM THE YONDER

A Collection of Horror from Around the World

Volume I

War Monkey Publications, LLC
Orem, Utah

©2020 War Monkey Publications, LLC

First Print, 2020

Cover Art by MtPArt
SelfPubBookCovers.com/ MtPArt

ISBN 978-1-7323662-4-4 (Paperback Cover)
ISBN 978-1-7323662-5-1 (ePub)

Library of Congress Control Number:2019921151

www.warmonkeypublications.com

TABLE OF CONTENTS

A NOTE FROM THE EDITOR

The idea for this anthology came about during a discussion with fellow horror enthusiasts. What would you really like to read? What would just be plain fun to read? How about a fiction anthology based on real tall-tales and legends? Other writers' perspectives and takes of existing spookiness. And thus, FROM THE YONDER was born.

Working on this anthology has been a real joy. Our readers were absolutely thrilled with the quality and craft of the submissions. And I loved them as well. I am still in final edits and our readers are already bugging me to continue this with future anthologies along the same "theme".

It is my sincere hope that the readers of this anthology enjoy it as much as I have.

Sincerely,

Joshua P. Sorensen

AUTHOR BIOS

L.F. FALCONER- L.F. Falconer is a lifelong resident of northern Nevada where she enjoys exploring the back roads, ghost towns, and the lonely places. An Indie author of dark fiction, she is a member of High Sierra Writers and has published seven novels and one collection of short stories. Her work has appeared in *Weirdbook Magazine* and *Shallow Waters Flash Fiction Anthology, Volume 4.* Discover more at www.lffalconer.com

LINDA KAY HARDIE- Recently Linda Kay Hardie has had stories published in A MURDER OF CROWS (Darkhouse Books, 2019) and STRANGE STORIES VOL. 1 (Forty-Two Books, 2019). Linda is the author of the picture book LOUIE LARKEY AND THE BAD DREAM PATROL (Moon Mountain Pub., 2001). Other credits include an essay in the book CAT WOMEN: FEMALE WRITERS ON THEIR FELINE FRIENDS and pieces in national magazines CAT FANCY and CHILE PEPPER. She is a professional member of SCBWI and of International Cat Writers Association, and holds a Master's Degree in English (Creative Writing). Her writing has won awards from the Cat Writers Association, the Association for California School Administrators, the California

Association of Community Colleges, and more. She won her first writing trophy in fifth grade, with first place for an essay on fire safety.

Linda Kay Hardie has been featured on the Food Network about the National Chicken Cooking Contest, for which she was the Nevada winner in 2001. She is also the Spam Cooking Champion for Nevada (yes, the tasty treat canned mystery meat). Linda been a disk jockey and newspaper reporter. A lifelong book lover, she is now an adjunct professor teaching English composition and core humanities to unwilling students in Reno, Nevada, where she lives with Abyssinian cats.

K.N. JOHNSON- K.N. Johnson's story "Frigid" won a Mythraeum contest for its haunting take on an artist obsessed with ice and one woman. "Frigid" was developed into a short film by Loste Films. Her dark non-fiction has appeared in various literary magazines and anthologies. She spends her days as a healthcare research specialist while studying psychology and weekends with her family, cats, and true crime films and podcasts. She's known to take too many photos during legend trips and ghost investigations. Follow her writing at www.facebook.com/knjohnsonauthor/

SHASHI KADAPA- Based in Pune, India, Shashi Kadapa is the managing editor of ActiveMuse, a journal of literature. His short stories appeared in anthologies of Casagrande Press, Alien Dimensions #11, Agorist Writers, Escaped Ink, War Monkey, Verses of Silence, Spadina Literary Review, and others. He has written for the The Times of India and Debonair. Shashi is working on a book of short stories and a novel.

C.R. LANGILLE- C.R. Langille spent many a Saturday afternoon watching monster movies with his mother. It wasn't long before he started crafting nightmares to share with his readers. An avid hunter and amateur survivalist, C.R. Langille incorporates the Utah outdoors in many of his tales. He is an affiliate member of the Horror Writer's Association, a member of the League of Utah Writers, and received his MFA: Writing Popular Fiction from Seton Hill University.

MIKE MARCUS- Mike Marcus lives in Pittsburgh, Pa., with his wife, Amy, and dog, Millie. A graduate of Frostburg State University in Frostburg, Md., Mike is a U.S. Army veteran from Mechanicsville, Md. Mike's short story "Ale for Humanity" appeared in Second Round: Return to the Ur-Bar, published in 2019 by Zombies Need Brains, LLC. Mike is currently working on his first novel. Follow Mike on Twitter @MikeMarcus77

SERGIO PALUMBO- Sergio is an Italian public servant and Law School graduate.

He is co-Editor, with Michele DUTCHER, of the Steampunk Anthology "Steam-powered Dream Engines", published in March 2018 and the Sci-Fi/Fantasy Anthology "Fantastical Savannahs and Jungles" released in 2019, both by Rogue Planet Press.

His Historical/Horror screenplay, "Tophet- An Ancient Evil", won an Honorable Mention at The 2018 International Horror Hotel Award in Richfield, Ohio.

His work, in both Italian and English, has been published in over 100 various anthologies throughout the World. He has published a Fantasy Role-Playing illustrated Manual, War Blades.

Sergio expects several dozen more publications in 2020/2021.

A listing of his publications, and some (free) flash fiction by him can be found at: http://www.aphelion-webzine.com/index.html

He is also a scale modeler whose dioramas have been shown in various Italian (scale model) magazines and internationally online. The internet site of his Model Club "La Centuria": www.lacenturia.it

JOSHUA P. SORENSEN- Joshua P. Sorensen is from Orem, Utah (United States). He travels extensively, inspiring him to write poetry and short fiction. His other loves include history, nature, and all things geek.

His Amazon profile can be found at:
http://amazon.com/author/joshuapsorensen/
His much neglected poetry blog can be found on
Facebook: @SorensenVagabondWriter
He can be found on Twitter @SorensenWriter

R. B. SWALLOW- This is R.B. Swallow's debut
publication. She absolutely loves horror, hockey, and
heavy metal. On most nights, she can be found
wrapped in a blanket in front of a roaring fire with her
two cats and a peppermint snuggler.

THE QUICK

Some things are full of mystery.
Some mysteries aren't good.

WILD THINGS

by L.F. Falconer

Bicuspids, incisors, canines, molars—distinctly human teeth strategically placed as balancing shims amid the precarious tower of stacked stones. Someone spent a lot of time putting this one together, Arlena thought. A lot more than the first cairn she'd passed on the other side of the hill. That one had simply been one rock placed atop another, six stones in all. Despite the grisly addition of teeth that the previous one lacked, this one was rather impressive, about four feet tall and filled with nearly impossible angles, flat rocks atop round ones, large upon small, in a wide range of colors. It could almost count as a work of art. So why spoil it with the bizarre addition of teeth?

Without thinking, she rubbed at the phantom ache in her jaw. It wasn't that long ago she'd had her wisdom teeth extracted. "Don't worry," Dr. Wong had assured her, "you'll still be wise." He was always full of lame jokes. Dentists must truly struggle for their humor. And what do they do with the teeth they pull? Use them to build cairns when out hiking?

Arlena backed off, away from the bizarre cairn, a knot twisting her gut, and she was grateful for Steve's service pistol at her hip. He'd be pissed if he knew she had it, always terrified it might fall into the wrong hands. But whose hands could it fall into out here?

All she'd wanted was to harvest some of the gooseberries that grew prolifically at Big Dens Creek to make a few jars of the jam she favored. It'd been years since she'd had any. Steve had refused to come with her, yet didn't think she should come alone, and had tried everything he could to dissuade her, insistent she stay near camp and fish with him.

"I'll be gone an hour, tops," she'd told him. "It's midweek and off season. No one'll be there."

"A Wilderness Area is meant for preservation, Arlena."

"I'm not going to rape the land."

"But you'd be stealing food from the indigenous species."

"I am an indigenous species."

"Your native blood notwithstanding, no one's above the law. You need to respect the wild things."

"What are you going to do? Arrest me?"

He'd fingered the weirdly etched, bloodstone cabochon that dangled from the chain around his neck, then fixed her under his steely, blue-eyed stare. "If you force my hand, I will."

"Screw you and your damn job." Arlena had gathered the dog, her day pack, a bucket, and the spare set of keys, taking off in the truck to leave him at the tent, alone and fuming. He hadn't pursued her on the four-wheeler, so she assumed he'd gotten a grip and would get over it. Either that or she'd be put into handcuffs when she got back to camp.

She just needed to break free. To enjoy the outdoors again. To not be shackled by all his damn "rules." To relive warm spring afternoons picking wildflowers (illegal, Steve says) or cool autumn mornings picking berries (also illegal, Steve says) for jams and jellies like she'd done with her mom and her mom's mom, learning of the old ways, ways of sustenance, of survival.

Staring again at the teeth in the cairn, she shuddered, cannily surveying her surroundings. She'd never ventured this deep into the Desatoya Range before. And she had broken one of Steve's cardinal rules when she'd strayed from the established path on the other side of the hill. She'd even far exceeded what her mom had always referred to as the safety zone at Big Dens Creek. Every time they'd come to the Dens to pick pine nuts or berries when Arlena was a child, her mom had always planted the fear of a mountain lion encounter solidly into her mind. Add to that her grandmother's old Shoshone legends and Arlena had never dared wander too far from her mother's side. "Se-da-e," Grandmother called this mountain range. Not Desatoya. Se-da-e. The first name, before the white man came. "Se-da-e," Grandmother would say. "No good. There are other mountains. Good mountains. Se-da-e," she would shake her head and scowl, "No good. No good."

Her dog, on the other hand, could not be convinced of the dangers, either real or mythical. Paco had taken off like a shot after a jackrabbit, disappearing over the crest of the hill flanking the creek. When he failed to return after nearly an hour, Arlena had had no choice but to go in search. At the truck she'd exchanged her bucket, filled with gooseberries, for her day pack which contained a small supply of protein snacks and bottled water. After pulling Steve's pistol out of the glove box, she'd sent him a quick text: "I'll be late getting back. Paco disappeared. Gone looking," inserting several heart emojis to help soften his anger at her defiance.

When they'd met at a symposium at the University of Nevada two years ago, she was thrilled to find an outdoorsy guy who wasn't a hard-core hunter, but lately she'd been having a lot of second thoughts. Mostly due to his strict adherence to certain rules of conduct, the most stringent being: Stay on the trails and respect the wild things. There are some places man is not meant to intrude. One small bucket of berries wasn't going to throw the entire ecosystem out of balance; and she'd had enough of his over-the-top, restrictive environmentalism. At times she felt like he cared more about ecosystems than he did about her. Every time they went camping or hiking, his Senior Wildlife Agent persona kicked into high gear.

She was currently stuck camping out here with him for four more days. She'd wait until they got home before breaking things off.

Locking the vehicle, she'd taken off on the dog's last known trail.

Reaching the crest of the first hill, she'd scanned the surrounding canyons, the slopes here steep and rugged. Humping over hills at 6000 feet was nothing to spit at and it had been months since she'd last done any serious hiking. Already her legs were feeling the burn. A light northern breeze chilled the pre-autumn air. She took several long drinks from a bottle of water and wished she'd brought a sweatshirt.

In the far distance, she'd caught the faintest hint of barking. She stowed the bottle back into her day pack and swiftly descended the hillside in pursuit. For the past three years, Paco, her little lifesaver, had been the love of her life. She'd never forget the look in his eyes the day she'd rescued the terrier-mixed mutt from the city pound the day he was slated for euthanasia. But the dog had rescued her as much as she'd rescued him. After her mom had been killed in a car accident, he'd given her something to cling to in life. A reason to go on.

Catching the hint of another bark, she continued on the dog's trail.

Nearly hidden amid the sagebrush and rose briars of the first canyon beyond Big Dens, she encountered a dry creek bed. And the first cairn. Not unusual. Many hikers used them as path markers when they strayed from the established trails. Other than its odd location, she didn't give it a single thought, not until she'd come upon this second one in the next canyon. This one with teeth. Out in the open, as a cairn should be. Yet there was no evidence of a trail nearby, so why was it here? And why the heck did it have teeth?

Perhaps she should turn back. Eventually Paco would find his way back to the truck, wouldn't he? Probably. Maybe. Maybe not. His barks sounded so far away.

A distant rumble drifted down the canyon wall and Arlena glanced skyward. White puffball clouds drifted against the blue and showed little threat of an imminent thunderstorm. The rumble sounded again, morphing into a steady pulse, like that of a distant heartbeat, haunting and foreign. Arlena shivered and took a step back, staring at the steep canyon walls.

Within moments, the drumming petered out like ripples in a pond and mountain silence settled back in.

"Paco!" she shouted, trepidation raising the timbre of her voice. Putting her fingers to her lips, she released a long, shrill whistle.

From somewhere beyond the canyon wall came a faint bark. She couldn't readily pinpoint the direction. Arlena surveyed the rough, craggy cliffsides towering in burnt umber like stalwart sentries, tufts of sagebrush and Indian tea sprouting within shallow pockets of soil. The only way to get to the top of the canyon would be to go downhill until she reached the origin of the outcropping.

Pushing her way through the thickets that choked the narrow gorge, she finally reached the point where the basalt uplift merged into earth. Measuring her pace, Arlena began the steep, upwards climb, low-cut hiking boots crunching loudly in the silence over the gravelly incline, back and forth in a zig-zag ascent through the sage and rabbit brush. She skirted around a few straggling boulders painted in black lichens with bright patches of yellow and tangerine. Sparse junipers crept up the hillside. A catbird mewed in the distance. Nearer to the crest, the pinions began to dominate and though the forest wasn't thick, it was absorbent enough to swallow most noise beyond the mournful, soughing wind that swept through the spiny branches. Grandmother had called that the spirit song of the trees, and sometimes she would sing along, encouraging Arlena to sing as well. Mom thought it all nothing but silliness, so never joined in. After Grandmother died, Arlena no longer tried to sing with the trees, however she always found their songs to be a source of peace.

Emerging into a small clearing near the top, she put her fingers to her lips again, letting loose another whistle, then held still in the hush. After a few moments, she whistled again. To her surprise, it echoed back. No—not an echo. Though similar to her own, it was distinctly different. Another whistle followed in the distance and her shiver raced all the way from head to heel. Guardedly, she rested her hand upon the butt of the pistol holstered at her hip. She'd heard a whistle like that before—not here in the Desatoyas, but last summer when she and Steve hiked the Toiyabe Crest Trail. Steve had recognized the whistle right away. Mountain lion. They had shared its territory for at least three days of their five-day hike. Although they never caught a glimpse of the cat, Arlena had no doubt it had seen them. She could sense it. With the aid of Steve's knowledge, it hadn't taken her long to learn to recognize the evidence of a cat's presence: the spoor, tracks, caterwauls. The chirps. The whistles.

The pines on the hillside above formed a ragged sawtooth edge before the backdrop of the dark, twin peaks of Desatoya, like a pair of sullen, barren spinsters brooding against the sky. "No good," Grandmother's voice echoed in Arlena's mind. "No good."

There are some places man is not meant to intrude. And other than Steve, who knew of these places better than the First People? Surely, they didn't dub this range Se-da-e without good reason. Then again, Grandmother's tales, while entertaining, were impossible to believe. Tales of the devious trickster, Coyote, who had put an end to eternal life. Or the Nimerigar, an evil, violent race of cannibalistic little people. And who could forget the infamous Water Babies, whose cries lured people into a watery grave? Silly superstitions, her mom had called them. Grandmother gave them far more merit.

Yet mountain lions were real. That was a danger Arlena could wrap her fears around.

In the distance came the bark of a dog, jarring Arlena back to the task at hand. She could swear it had come from behind her, but when another bark sounded, the direction was definitely forward. After taking a long drink of water, she continued her overland trek, pushing deeper into the wilderness.

Near the next sloping saddle the trees thinned, revealing the crowning crags that covered the hillcrest in Desatoya's shadow. Arlena stopped to catch her breath. From here the view opened up, a clear vista of the majestic Toiyabe Range to the east and fifty miles to the west, a horizon line jagged with the Stillwater Range. The kind of view she would never tire of, revealing the vast open lands her grandmother's people had once freely inhabited.

Arlena slaked her thirst and pulled her cell phone from her day pack. No reception. No messages. No voice mails. Steve was probably chomping at the bit by now. She'd never hear the end of it.

"Stay on the established trails. Respect the wild things," she grumbled. "Four more days. Then he's out of my life for good."

With a sigh, she tucked the phone away and took another drink of water, listening to the quiet. The spirit song of the trees. The chit of a sparrow. The distant mew of a catbird. Again, she thought she could hear a faint, rhythmic heartbeat. And off to the left, a bark. Louder than before. Much closer.

"Paco!" she shouted, spurred into action, crossing over the rocky detritus and dodging the interloping pines as she made her way across the saddle until she peered down at the aspen-filled canyon below. She gazed back, gauging the distance she'd already covered in the last three hours. It'd be near nightfall by the time she got back. Steve was going to be so, so pissed.

The desolation—the aloneness was palpable. She could nearly taste it, like bile upon her tongue. She emptied another water bottle and rubbed at her aching calves before moving on.

"Dammit, Paco." She worked her way down the steep slope toward the chattering aspens already beginning to yellow for the autumn season. "Oh, I just love chasing my dog through the wilderness, said no one, ever. I swear, this is the last canyon. If you don't show your face soon, I'm just going to head back and leave you to fend for yourself." An empty threat made of frustration. She'd never abandon her little lifesaver, and knew she was closing in. She wouldn't give up now.

Halfway down the slope she stopped at a low wire cable that stretched across the terrain upon short metal posts. It wasn't completely closed off like a plant study area, the cable was certainly no deterrent to animals, big or small. This was meant only to keep people at bay, evident by the numerous signs posted along its length, proclaiming: "Protected Habitat. Do Not Enter."

The eerie sensation of being watched tightened her stomach. Her pulse raced, but not from the strain of the hike. Were there cameras positioned around, monitoring the area—spying to see who "respected the wild things" and who didn't? But the sensation felt more personal, as if actual eyes were upon her. Much like it felt for three days on the Toiyabe Crest Trail last summer.

Trying to spot the tawny coat of a big cat, she scanned the rocky ridge crowning the peak above, a peak still dwarfed by the imposing Desatoya twins beyond, naked above the tree line. She could detect no movement. Hear no signs. Nothing but stillness and silence. Not even a breath of a breeze to sing the song of the trees. No birds. No cat whistles. No dogs barking in the distance. No faint engine whine of Steve on the four-wheeler coming to reprimand her. It was as if the world had stood still for a moment to catch its breath. Or to sleep.

A bone-chilling screech of a hawk on the hunt shattered the silence. Startled, with the spell now broken, Arlena studied the prohibited canyon beyond the cable. Her dog was down there. Somewhere. Taking a deep breath, she stepped over the cable and proceeded down the slope.

A running creek babbled through the whispering aspen leaves and she came to a dead halt. Upon a level swath of grass, an elaborate, towering cairn stood nearly as tall as she, the stones shimmed not with teeth, but short, slender bones. Warily, she leaned in for a closer look. Animal, or human? Her blood turned to ice. First teeth, now bones. Who built these things? And why? These were no trail markers. They looked sinister. A warning of some type? Or maybe just some wildland advocate's weird way of trying to scare people away from the protected habitat? To keep them on the established trails?

Pocked with tiny caves, the rocky canyon wall on the opposite side of the creek loomed above the golden aspens. Sweeping off those walls, a ghostly, bone-chilling, banshee wail echoed through. The hairs rose on her arms, her neck.

Mountain lion! Unmistakably so. Though late in the season, a mating call, which meant there could be more than one cat in the vicinity.

Not far down the tree-cloaked canyon came the bark of a dog, and she wheeled around. Paco was close. She called out to him, again, and waited. The dog barked twice yet didn't sound any closer.

She was hesitant to enter the trees. It wasn't just the possibility of encountering a big cat. It was the odd cairns. It was the silence. The aloneness. The preternatural chill in the air. Her trespass onto forbidden ground.

Knowing she'd probably not have reception down in this canyon, she pulled out her phone, checking the signal strength anyway before she snapped a few photos of the bizarre cairn beside her. Steve might know more about it than she. Why hadn't she thought to take pictures of the previous one—the one with teeth?

Downstream in the aspens came another bark. Arlena shrugged off her day pack, swapping out her empty water bottle for a fresh one. She'd refill the empty one with creek water before heading back on the long trek to the truck. A trek she didn't look forward to. It might've only been a mile or two as the crow flies but crossing over steep terrain was strenuous. Her legs were going to hurt for days.

Leaving the morbid cairn behind, she turned her back to it and headed into the trees.

The riparian air was dank compared to the dry pinion forest beyond, the white-barked aspens unmaligned by the old etchings of Basque sheep herders—this deep wilderness as primitive and pristine as it gets. "A place man should not intrude upon," Steve would've reminded her even though he was miles away. Yet, she had intruded, and something about this area continually reminded her of that transgression. The desolation ran deep. She was hesitant to call out to Paco again, to smirch the peculiar silence. Even though armed, a heightened sense of vulnerability encompassed her. Desatoya. Se-da-e. No good.

Ducking beneath low-hanging limbs, she sidled around the stern clumps of nettles and wild parsley, down the creek side toward the direction Paco had last been heard. Coming to a dead halt, she stared at the tracks in the mud, then knelt to inspect them more closely. Too big to belong to Paco, the pads bore three lobes instead of two, with toes shaped like teardrops. Clearly, the tracks of a mountain lion. And not far away, the track of a barefoot child. A shudder raced up her arms and into her spine, a prickle like spiders crawling right out the base of her skull.

How old these tracks were, she did not know but they were new enough to still be sharply defined. Creeping into the silence, the aspen leaves chattered, whispering like soft voices, imparting the spirit song of the trees, more malignant than peaceful. Through the canopy, the screech of a hawk ghosted down. A distant catbird mewed. And from downstream, beyond the clusters of rose briars and sage, came a whistle. Although it might sound human, she knew it belonged to a cat.

Ever so slowly, she unholstered the pistol and released the safety, glancing down once more at the child's footprint in the mud. Had some diehard hiker brought a toddler up here? No matter how unlikely it seemed, it wasn't beyond the realm of possibilities.

A peripheral flash of movement to the right caused her to wheel about, raising and aiming the gun. Flickering like candle flames, light and shadow danced through the canopy. All she could see were the trees, the shrubbery and grass, the trilling creek tumbling over its stony bed. A scampering ground squirrel. Guardedly, she lowered her weapon.

A long, loud chirp, like the call of a large bird, squealed through the wooded gorge, followed by another short, shrill whistle.

Arlena shivered. The nearness of the cat was a clear danger and if she had the sense of a horse, she'd back away and head for open ground. But how could she leave Paco behind when she'd finally gotten this close? She couldn't. Not now. Not when she knew there was a killer twice his size in the vicinity.

Keeping her gun hand on point, she cautiously continued downstream on stealthy footsteps, glancing over her shoulder now and then, scanning her entire surroundings. Another track in the mud caught her eye. Dog or cat, this one she couldn't discern, for it was smudged too much.

She peered up at the canyon wall, the dark volcanic face dotted with holes of various diameters and depths. For an instant, her footsteps faltered.

Something had moved inside one of the small caverns. A rodent? More likely a bird. Such a high den would be fairly protected against predators, higher up the cliff face was a definite aerie. Perhaps hawks and eagles weren't the only ones to know the value of cliffside dwelling.

Resuming her path, she glanced back over her left shoulder, deciding that from now on, Paco would have to be tethered on their outings. That's all there was to it. She was not going to chase him down every time he took it into his head to run off.

The trees clustered tightly in the canyon, the sun stabbing light through in sporadic rays, illuminating the dying blades of grass on the creekbank. Another bark. Much closer this time. Arlena quickened her pace. The subsequent barks immediately morphed into yips of fear or pain, barely muted by the trilling, swift-flowing creek. Jinking around the brambles and branches on the creek bank, Arlena clamped the pistol tightly in preparation to shoot the cat, the dog's yelps growing more high-pitched and desperate with every harried step she took.

A high-pitched squeal. Then…

Silence.

"No, no, no," Arlena guttered, rushing faster down the rocky bank, her heart thumping, boots beating against the dirt. Skirting around a thick clump of rose briar near a roaring cascade, her feet skidded over loose shale on the short, steep slope. Her butt smacked against the ground and sliding down, she tried but couldn't stop her momentum, ramming full force into a close-set row of wooden spikes entrenched at the bottom of the rise. One spike plunged into her right ankle just above her boot top. Another speared through the denim of her jeans, impaling her left calf.

A searing yowl tore from her throat. She yanked free. Dropping the pistol, she locked her hands onto her wounds. Tear-filled eyes stared up at the animal on the creek bank. Not Paco. Not a cat. A gray fox. No, not a fox. Merely the pelt of a fox with the head attached, much like one of those horrid vintage stoles women wore in the '40s. Only instead of wrapping around the shoulders, this one's head rested atop the head of a child. No—even viewed through a veil of tears, it was clearly no child. It was a man, a small man, perhaps no more than eighteen inches in height, clad only in a leather loin cloth, a bloodstone necklace, and the pelt of the fox. He had bare feet. Small, bare feet.

His skin was a deep, russet brown, his charcoal eyes almost owlish above a long, hooked nose centered upon a squat, flat face. Blood red lips curled into a shark-like smile, revealing teeth of mustard yellow, long and sharp. Perfect for ripping and tearing.

Eyes gleaming with sadistic pleasure, the small creature stepped forward, leaned in…and barked.

Braying laughter rose up from all sides. Throbs of pain clouded Arlena's vision as the throng of tiny men stepped free of the shadows.

Nimerigar! Grandmother's little people.

Se-da-e. No good.

Dressed in fox, badger, jackrabbit, marmot, and fisher skins, all were armed with primitive spears or bows, arrows tipped with sharp obsidian points. One of the men chirped. Another whistled. One screeched like a hawk while another quietly mewed like a catbird in the distance. Again, the gray fox before her barked, then released a high-pitched yelp like a dog in pain. The clan laughed and whispered amongst themselves, their words indecipherable, but as a chorus altogether they sounded much like the spirit song of the trees, though far from peaceful. The malevolence within their laughter was clearly understood.

Across the creek sat women and children, lightly beating the skins of deep, wooden drums with bones, the rhythm steady as a heartbeat. In their midst, shining within a shaft of sunlight near the base of the cliff, stood another cairn. One made entirely of blood-stained bones. Capped with a human skull. Not small. Not one of their own.

Arlena glanced back at the gun on the ground beside her. Pulling her right hand away from her wounded leg, she grabbed for the weapon. Instantly, her hand was pinned to the ground, pierced clean through, the arrow not much bigger than a bamboo skewer. A scream tearing from her very core, she yanked the hand free from the earth, blood oozing from her palm in drops upon the ground below.

The drums beat louder. Faster. Laughter bore down on her ears like a hammer on anvil, her hand pulsing in agony while streams of fire coursed through her punctured ankle and leg.

Grasping onto her right wrist with her left hand, she struggled up to a sitting position.

The surrounding Nimerigar stepped in closer, spears raised, arrows nocked.

The drums beat faster.

Arlena's hand tingled, a million needle points pricking beneath her flesh from the palm outward. Gritting her teeth, she grabbed onto the arrow point and yanked downward as hard as she could, a guttural cry clogging her throat as the small arrow shaft ripped through, her flesh tearing at the palm and the back of her hand. The remnants of two jagged holes streamed blood.

The Nimerigar chanted in unison with the steadily increasing drumbeats.

Arlena scrambled for the pistol with her left hand. Grasping onto it, she raised it awkwardly, shakily. Through a blur, she aimed at the gray fox.

"Stay back." The warning gurgled from the back of her throat.

The gray fox deliberately stepped forward.

Arlena pulled the trigger.

A deafening roar assaulted her ears, the recoil flipping the gun from her unsteady grip.

The gray fox dropped to the ground, the remains of his head spattered across the rocks behind him, the hole in his head staining the earth red. Like a pack of coyotes in moonlight, a shrill and mournful kip and ki-yi howl rose from the surrounding tribesmen.

On the shale incline behind her came a lumbering rumble. A bark. A low curse, "Godammit."

Arlena's quick glance backward turned into a deluge of relief.

"Steve!" she cried out. "Thank God."

With Paco leashed in tight control at his side, Steve revealed his bloodstone necklace to the angry tribe, bringing them to a swift halt. He then rushed forward and snatched up his fallen pistol.

"How many times have I told you to stay on the trails? To respect the wild things," he shouted, shambling back toward the incline, Paco fighting against the taut leash. "Even your dog had enough sense to stay near the truck." Forcing the dog to remain at his side, he began to ascend the slope.

"Help me," Arlena reached out with her bleeding hand. "I can't walk."

"I tried to catch you before you got this far. But it's too late." He continued forcing the dog up the incline.

"What? Wait! You can't just leave me!"

The drumbeats roared.

"No one's above the law, Arlena." At the top of the incline, Steve aimed the gun in her direction. "I'm sorry. They're an endangered species. You're not. But I won't let you suffer."

A rain of small arrows pierced Arlena's flesh The gun blast rang off the canyon walls. As her pain washed out onto a black, black sea, in the unfathomable distance, she heard the barking of a dog.

BEWARE THE WATER BABIES
OF PYRAMID LAKE

by Linda Kay Hardie

Marcus goosed the cruise control a few more m.p.h. up to 75 as he passed a speed limit sign sporting a giant 55. There wasn't any traffic on the Pyramid Lake Highway this Tuesday afternoon, and he enjoyed zooming along like a low-flying aircraft. He felt his neck and shoulder muscles loosening as he let Reno eat his dust.

Once he hit the reservation, Marcus slowed down to the tribal speed limit. He knew the drive to the fishing lodge would be longer, but the tribal cops didn't mess around. Not that the Nevada state troopers did, but Marcus felt he had a fighting chance to see them before they saw him. Besides, he could see the sights better at a slower speed. Marcus preferred the wild and empty Pyramid Lake to the tourist-infested

Lake Tahoe. You could really get away from things out here.

His phone buzzed. His wife's picture flashed on the screen, and Marcus hit ignore. Let her stew longer. His good mood teetered, and he nearly tumbled back into anger. How dare she call so soon to apologize? He was still angry about the incident that morning. He glanced at his hands on the steering wheel. His knuckles were starting to show bruises. Bitch.

Driving 45, he was better able to feel the temperature on this early September day: a warm, pre-fall afternoon. The joke in Washoe County is that the temperature could go from 95 to 55 like it saw a trooper. Marcus, who grew up in San Diego, felt this was a typical So-Cal sort of day, with a high in the middle 70s. But Washoe would assert itself in the evening, with a low around 40 predicted. Great fishing weather, even though he couldn't catch the Lahontan cutthroat trout at this time of year. And he couldn't catch the endangered cui-ui at any time. At least there was the Sacramento perch available now. Good eating, if his wife didn't fuck up cooking it. Her heart was never in it because she didn't like fish.

*****

Usually, Marcus slept well at the Crosby Lodge, but this time noises kept him awake. At first, he thought it was cats fighting, but he soon realized it was children playing. He looked at his phone. What were kids doing outside after 11 on a weeknight? Little monsters shrieking outside his window.

Kids were always a problem. His own son was three years old already and still crying like a baby. Fucking wimp. Marvin should have been toilet trained by now, but Deborah was always coddling him, letting him get away with shit. Like last night. What Marvin needed was a good smack upside the head, and Marcus gave him that. Stupid brat began to wail, and Deborah yelled, so Marcus smacked her, too. That shut her up, but the boy only cried harder.

"Shut him up," Marcus had said. "Get him out of my sight."

Now Marcus sat up in bed. The little bastards outside were crying. He laid back down. He was never going to get to sleep. But he did. He even slept past his alarm at 5:15 and woke up with the sun at 6:45. A late start to today's fishing.

Walking from his cabin to the lodge, Marcus could smell buttermilk pancakes as well as coffee. Might as well eat a real breakfast since he'd already fucked up the morning. He turned on the charm for the waitress, because he might get an extra piece of toast or strip of bacon. She responded to his winning smile and compliments by making sure his coffee cup never ran low. And he got an extra pancake once he'd finished the two that she'd initially brought him.

"Say, Anna," he said, flashing his best grin. Her name was on a badge on her ample chest. "What's with the kids playing outside late last night? I heard them past 11."

Anna's smile dropped off her face. "There aren't any children around here," she said. "And children on this reservation don't go out that late at night anyway."

Marcus let his charming mask fall for a moment. But he pasted the smile back on.

"What did I hear then? I thought at first it was cats."

A double ding from the kitchen interrupted Anna's reply. "Just a moment," she said, her face still serious, and she pretty much ran to the kitchen to get the order. But she returned after delivering eggs and bacon to the ugly tourist couple. She'd brought a second cup of coffee (his was still full and hot) and sat down across from him. She took a gulp of her coffee.

"Long ago, back when the cui-ui were plentiful," she began. It sounded sing-song, like it was rehearsed or something that was used a lot, like fairy tales starting with "once upon a time."

Anna told him a long and bizarre story of ancient times before the white man came to Nevada. There was a man of the Numu – "the people," Anna said, "that is, the cui-ui eating Paiute" – who fell in love with a mermaid-serpent from Pyramid Lake. He took her back to the village so they could get married, but the people were frightened by her appearance, her fish scales and gills and sharp teeth. They drove her away, back to the lake. She cursed them and she cursed the lake.

Things seemed back to normal, but one night a young woman feeding her child on the shores of the lake had occasion to put her baby down and step away for a moment. A serpent slithered out of the water and gobbled up the baby, then took its form. The woman turned back and picked up the serpent in the baby's form and put it to her breast. But when it opened its mouth, the woman saw a dozen pointed teeth. She screamed, tossing the water baby to the ground. The baby, now with sharp claws on its hands and feet, ran to the lake, disappearing in the depths.

"Since that time, the water babies, complete with scales and gills, haunt the lake. Some say they are the children of the mermaid and the man of the Numu," Anna said. "Whoever hears the water babies is cursed by bad luck. He who sees them will die."

She stood up, set down Marcus's check, and disappeared into the kitchen.

Marcus was stunned. But he shook his head and came to his senses. Fairy tales! He'd never heard before that Pyramid Lake had little monster mermaid babies in it. Some asshole public relations agency probably created the whole story to try to drum up interest in this lake whose tourism paled in comparison to Lake Tahoe's.

He wrote his cabin number on the check and signed it, leaving it on the table.

Marcus spent the day fishing on the lake. He didn't have any luck the first couple hours, but after he realized he was irritable because of that story Anna had told, he cracked open a beer from his cooler and calmed himself down. He didn't care that it was only 10 o'clock. That was the beauty of fishing, that you could have a beer without worrying about the time. No one to nag you.

Even though he composed himself and relaxed, he still didn't catch anything. That wasn't normal. Bad luck. He had a momentary twinge when that phrase landed in his brain. No, he wasn't having bad luck because he'd heard some mythical water babies crying during the night. The conditions on Pyramid Lake, like the weather, could change without a moment's notice. That's all it was.

His phone buzzed and Deborah's picture showed up again. How dare she take this much time getting back to him to apologize? Her smile on her photo made him want to punch her in the mouth again. His anger flooded back. She was still taunting him, trying to make him lose control. He hit ignore. It was only two o'clock, but the mood was broken and he didn't feel like fishing anymore today.

*****

Thursday started off much better. He woke to his alarm at 5:15 and was out on the lake by 5:45, an hour before dawn, when it was permitted to start fishing. No sign of the sun yet, just a lighter shade of teal in the eastern sky. At first, it was peaceful in the dark, with the occasional quiet plash of a jumping fish. Then he began to hear voices. Not other fishermen. Children's voices. Chattering like magpies. But not birds. He couldn't quite make out words, and then the sounds turned to laughter.

Deborah. Somehow, she'd set up the children's voices for him to hear, made up the story that the waitress told. She was exactly that devious. He pulled out his phone and punched in her number. She answered on the third ring.

"Mah-cuth," she lisped his name. Bitch was pretending her face was swollen. He hadn't hit her that hard. And that was her fault anyway for forgetting to fix his lunch on time. She had whined that she had to be on the phone with the pediatrician, but that was just an excuse for his hypochondriac son.

"You made up that water babies story, didn't you? You and some of your PR friends. You still talk to them behind my back, don't you? How did you do it, make the noises of the children?"

Deborah didn't say anything. Marcus prepared to yell at her, but he heard splashing along the side of the boat, and he saw a small hand with claws reach over the starboard gunwale. Then another. And another. Lots of clawed hands. Then small faces with sharp, grinning teeth appeared, and the water babies levered themselves into the boat. Seven small, scaly water babies, all staring at him.

Marcus dropped his phone and screamed.

"What is it?" Deborah's tinny voice was barely audible.

"Water babies! Go away!" he shouted. He waved his arms at them. They advanced on him, surrounding him in the small boat. The tiny razor claws grabbed at him, and tiny jaws full of razor teeth bit down on his ankles and wrists and thighs and stomach. The water babies began to chew and chew and chew. Marcus's screams became bloodcurdling. Blood filled the bottom of the boat, and it shorted out his phone.

The water babies chewed on Marcus until the screaming stopped. It took a long time. They leaned over the gunwale of the boat and made magpie noises to the water. A large serpent head appeared, and it tipped the boat over. The water babies laughed as they and what remained of Marcus fell into the cold and deep lake.

*****

Deborah called 911 and explained that her husband appeared to be in trouble on Pyramid Lake. The Washoe county 911 operator connected her with tribal police up at the lake, and they said they would investigate. She didn't mention what he said about water babies. It sounded like another one of his violent rants anyway.

The tribal police found Marcus's boat, tipped over in the lake. They said that sudden winds could tip over boats, especially if the fisherman had been drinking and stood up. They didn't mention the water babies either. Nor the claw marks on the side and bottom of the boat. Just another unlucky fisherman.

DARK OF THE NIGHT

by R. B. Swallow

The warm breeze of September brought the smell of pine to Sean as he stood looking over the quiet mountain meadow high in the Uintah mountains. The sun was just starting to dip below the crest of the west mountain peak turning the sky hues of pink and orange. The sight was breathtaking, yet, he felt a silent unease knowing what he faced in the night.

With the lowering of the sun came the rise of the bright harvest moon. The moonlight cast strange shadows on the ground, distorting his sight and tricking his depth perception.

Sean looked like some strange sort of medieval knight in chainmail and leather armor with swords strapped to his back. He had a belt with pouches that went around his waist for various odds and ends. A vial of holy water, a bag of silver shavings, a bag of herbs including wolfsbane and blessed thistle, and one small pouch that was empty except for bits of old dried wild flowers and faded yellow leaves given to him by a dear friend and lover a long time ago. He kept them in her memory as she was the one who taught him how to hunt. He shook his head, that was all in the past now.

Sean adjusted his small backpack with its attached quiver that held both arrows and bow. The steel arrowheads had a coating of silver making them deadly to both skinwalkers and lycans. Others like him hunted with loud guns and left bodies littering the forest floor. He used the one and only Native American ritual he knew to release their spirits and dispose of their empty flesh, Witch Fire. He respected the life he hunted, even if they turned into monsters who hunted savagely, leaving ruined bodies and ruined lives. Besides, tonight, he hunted a skinwalker, and skinwalkers don't respond to bullets.

His quarry has been spotted outside of Dark Canyon by Skinwalker Ranch and led him now to the central Uintah Mountains. Now that night had fallen fully and the moon was high above the cliffs, Sean scanned the valley, with its light tree cover, for sign of movement. He took in a chest full of air hoping to smell the scent of canine amongst the wood scent of the trees. The night was still and no movement met his acute sight. He would have to go down to the valley below, to where he had found the creature's den.

Sean straitened his greaves around his jeans and leather hiking boots, then tightened his hard leather bracers on his forearms, tying them down over his long sleeve AC/DC tee shirt. One last check on the buckles securing his armor and he felt ready to face the beast one more time. Sean learned long ago that the monsters he hunted could shred a man and did with great joy.

Sean had dark brown hair with a touch or gray at the temples. He had a muscular body from running the mountain trails carrying his arsenal on his back. He

47

had soft kind eyes but often had a touch of a smirk in his smile.

On nights like this he often wondered if she had more weapons and armor maybe she would not have disappeared into the night... but she chose only her bow and a single obsidian long knife. Sean shook his head to clear away the nightmarish memory. She was the one who brought him to her Navajo tribal elders and shaman. They taught to him the ritual for Witch Fire. Their sacred rituals were passed down through her tribe, so Sean had to suffer the ramifications for what was not his by birth. For him it meant he now had one bright blue eye, and his normal dark brown, with a scar under his new blue eye.

Sean's memory drifted to her more these crisp autumn nights. She disappeared in September and he always thought of her when the mountain nights started to run cold, turning one or two leaves yellow on the mountains. She hunted without protection save the black denim jeans, soft black doeskin shirt she wore, and his gift. He had made her a gift of hard leather greaves, bracers, and a hard leather breast plate with a coyote wearing raven feathers howling on the front, all in black and red, her favorites. She loved them and wore them at every hunt.

Sean silently crept down the deer path into the quiet tree line. Each footfall set deliberately to keep his passing unnoticed. He stopped many times, crouching behind a tree or bush, listening to the night sounds. He noted that an owl had found a vole and was eating it to his left. To his right, crickets chirped undisturbed by his passing or any other creature.

Further down the mountain a fox barked a warning cry then went suddenly silent. That was what Sean was waiting for, something bigger than a fox hunted this night. Sean could feel the presence of evil come the Native witch monster. To become a skinwalker you first had to have the magic in you. Then you had to be so evil and corrupt that you take a close family member's life. There was more to the ritual magic to become one, however Sean hated to think about it.

He crept silently on, keeping upwind of the den, choosing to come from the west side of the valley. He found a vantage point and hid until he could smell the rank scent or the creature coming through the trees, wet canine and viscera. He preferred not to get cornered inside the den, it blocked his way of retreating if he needed to get out fast. He waited until he could see it's eyes shining in the moonlight, burning red coals, and not the golden eyes of a wolf. The mountain meadow went silent with the presence of the massive predator.

The skinwalker was big, the largest misshapen monster Ian had seen in years. It's head easily came to Ian's shoulders. He was light gray with sharp yellow teeth in his great, snapping jaw. Blood still coated its powerful chest from the dead fox that now lay discarded in the trees.

Sean skillfully notched an arrow and pulled the bow string back slowly, relying on the patience of his arm to keep the bow string and his armor quiet. He sighted in the wolf-like creature, following his movements, anticipating which way he would jump at the sound of the arrows release. He drew in a breath and let it out as the arrow flew. As the skinwalker heard the twang of the arrow leaving the string, it jumped. The arrow skimmed off its ribs right under his vital organs. The silver would do its work, but slowly, he was in for one damn fight.

The Navajo witch roared at him and headed straight for his hiding spot. His breathing becoming labored from the silver, however, not enough to fell him in time.

Sean didn't have time to notch another arrow before the charging beast would be at his throat. He drew his sword and ran for more open ground. His breath came in sure measured draws and his legs flew quickly over the forest floor. Sean dodged trees and hurtled over small boulders and scrub oak bushes. The walker was so close behind Sean that he could smell his vile breath.

Sean dropped down suddenly behind a large boulder he had just hurtled over and, crouching, rounded the big rock to the other side. The wolf sailed past him into the trees. It was now a game of hide and seek. A very deadly game of hide and seek! Sean retraced his steps back along the trail for a little while until he came to a small copse of aspen trees. He wound his way in and around it as fast as he could while holding his weaponry close to his body, then again ran back up the trail toward the wolf and hid behind the boulder, quieting his ragged breathing. He knew the monster would hunt him through the trees slowing it to a crawl. Sean now had time to make his way to the clearing while the silver further poisoned the skinwalker.

The skinwalker finally caught Sean's scent and ran back down the trail to the copse of aspen trees. He slowed his pace as he wound his way cautiously through the trees, scenting the air as well as the ground. He could smell Sean in the vegetation, but he was weary of being hemmed in by the close trees. If

Sean were to strike at him, he could not maneuver enough to evade the blow.

As the massive misshapen wolf cautiously backed himself out of the closely growing trees, Sean dashed into the clearing he had spotted from the cliffs above. He stood in the middle, his shining long sword in front of him with his elbow bent and his right foot in front of the other. Sean quieted his mind and body, he watched and listened for the skinwalker's approach. He did not have to wait long. The night went still and the giant skinwalker slunk into the clearing with his head lowered, a low rumbling growl breaking the stillness.

The walker slowly slunk into the meadow, sizing Sean up. He prowled first to the right, then to the left, keeping his eyes on his prey the whole time. He roared a harrowing challenge that shocked the forest into palpable silence. He could smell Sean's fear in his sweat and hear his heartbeat just a little faster. He knew this hunter meant death for him with his silver arrows and his swords. He scented the air again and still could not smell any guns on this man. He smelled a whiff of something else though, something that tickled a memory in the back of his mind, wood smoke and burning sage. It sparked a feeling of rage in him and he charged forward.

Sean drew his other sword just as the skinwalker started to charge him. The skinwalker ran at him with his ears flat to his skull and chest close to the ground, speeding like a streak of light in the darkness. At the last second, he dodged to the right raking his teeth across Sean's lower thigh, just where the chainmail stopped. Sean cut a slice from the witch Native's flank as he tried to dodge and strike at the same time. This was not a new war he waged but one well practiced.

Instead of circling around, the walker flipped backwards suddenly, trying to catch Sean before he could bring his swords around. But Sean had expected him to do just that and raked the blade up across his ribs and under his leg. The witch Native howled his rage and pain! He sank to the ground collapsing back on his haunches, his eyes glowing a violent red in the darkness. Although no blood dripped from the cuts, the wounds were still real and painful. One last time, the skinwalker gathered his body under himself and sprang up to tear out Sean's throat. Sean stepped back with one foot and, with both swords, sliced sideways across the skinwalker's neck, cleaving his head from his body.

Inertia carried the head and body into Sean as blood finally splattered over his chest. The body of a tall well-muscled Navajo man slumped to the ground. He wore a wolfs head and his face was blackened with war paint. On his body he had filthy jeans and leather bracelets beaded with great care. Sean laid him on the ground with great care making sure to gather anything he wore and any bead that might have come loose putting them in his pockets. He gathered wood and placed it under him, then rocks to make a circle around the fire. He took out of his pouch a sprinkling of the wolf's bane and blessed thistle. He added some sage and tossed the dried herbs over the body. With great effort he called the Witch Fire and watched the man burn in blue flames. Sean wonder, as he watched the flames, why the walker didn't eat the fox, but instead he left it abandoned in the clearing.

Sean walked back to the den, the gash on this thigh slowed him down a little, the deadly chase through the night slowing him more. The den smelled of rotten meat and unwashed bodies, littered around the ground were bones, leaves, and pieces of animal pelts, the roof and sides of the cave were covered in greasy soot. A low growl rumbled up from the bowls of the cave where a fire glowed.

Sean made his way slowly in amid the dancing shadows cast by the uneven rock face and the firelight. Behind the fire lay a deep, black shadow that the fire could not penetrate. The shadow felt somehow cold and full of rage. As Sean stepped into the fire's light the shadow slowly dissipated. Another skinwalker walked slowly forward and sat on its hind legs. The Native witch cocked its head to the side, first one way, then the other. Sean felt like he was being thought about, not sized up, it was strange and out of place. It... she had to be very powerful to do such a ritual spell as that and to be so at ease with Sean standing armed ready to kill her. She was coal black with white spots about her ears and those burning red eyes, her body was much smaller than the man he killed, much more delicate. She bared her teeth at the man who had killed the other walker, saliva dripping from her sharp teeth with her lips curled away in a terrifying grimace.

She suddenly sprang up on her hind legs, lunging forward towards Sean, intent on tearing out his throat. Sean slashed a sword across her front legs as she pulled her head sharply back. She changed from wolf to woman, in that moment as her life blood flowed out of her. Sean cried out in rage and pain as his lost love fell to the earth in front of him. Sean held her as blood oozed out of her ruined arms. He screamed at her in confusion and rage. "How? How can you be the evil thing we hunted together?"

Her body became relaxed in his arms and Sean knew she was dying. His heart softened as he held her.

He knew she could deal death, why not kill in rage as well as in justice? He brought his lips to hers one last time as she went still, "Goodbye Shannon Coyote Feathers!" he tenderly brushed her matted hair away from her painted face. Sean laid her gently down on the cave floor and searched for wood and rocks for the witch fire ritual. A pit opened in his stomach as he found among the discarded bones and fur bits her leather bracers, breast plate, and greaves. He fingered the worn leather softly and laid them on her chest to burn with her.

Sean concentrated on the ritual, desiring to cleanse the entire cave of the evil and release her soul. He brought dry wood from the forest to create a huge fire. He used a pine bough and brushed all the bone and fur fragments into the pile to cleans the cave of all the evil memories and imprints. He set the stones in a circle around it tossing in whole branches of white sagebrush to chase the ghosts and spirits away.

Sean reverently chanted the ritual, quietly watching Shannon's large brown eyes as the blues flames began to lick up around her body. He could almost feel in his heart, one last time, the warm embrace of her arms around his back holding him to her. He could smell her scent. Doe skin and pine forest. He could taste her sweet breath as she kissed him one last time.

Then he felt the searing caress of the Witch Fire. Shannon had one dead hand clamped around his arm and had pulled him into the flame. Sean took in one last breath to scream, but the flames enveloped his lungs rendering him mute in his agony. He wrestled desperately with the corpse even as his cloths, skin, and hair burnt off his body. His chainmail melted into his flesh, fusing to his bones and boiling his blood inside him. With a last burst of blue- and white-hot flame, both bodies fell to ash that became sparkling dust, rising up into the night sky.

HUNTING SEASON

by Joshua P. Sorensen

The pick-up bounced along the dirt road. Even though it was well graded, it wasn't regularly traveled, and Charlie was still a bit drunk. The two drunks sitting in the bed hopped about with each jerk, yelling at him to slow down.

Charlie slammed to a stop and drifted to the side of the road. He had already turned off the Chevy's engine and dismounted when the sedan caught up with them. Three guys piled out of it as Charlie's passengers climbed over the tailgate.

"Show us the aliens, man," the driver of the other car hollered.

"Yeah, let's kick E.T.'s ass!"

Charlie smiled with pleasure. It was rare that anyone ever believed him about seeing UFO's up in the Santa Ynez Mountains, especially hovering over Gibraltar Reservoir. But he had found a willing audience at the El Rancho, a fly-by-night dive bar and one of the few places that still let him drink there.

These five drunks had happily followed him up into the hills to go on an alien hunt. He didn't recognize any of them. Henry, the bartender, had told them if they bought him a few drinks that Charlie would tell them all about his alien abduction. Which they did. And by the end of the night, they found themselves driving up a Forest Service road on the hunt for UFO's.

"I see them mostly by the dam. Just a little further up the road."

Charlie led his inebriated entourage along the dirt path to the dam. Once they got there, one of his companions waved his hands at the big parking lot at the top of the road.

"What the hell!?! Why didn't we just stop here?"

Through blurred memory, Charlie remembered his name was Dennis.

"I didn't want our headlights to give the aliens any warning. Or alert anyone that might be working tonight." He gestured to the pumping station just beyond the parking area.

He led them all out onto the catwalk that crossed the spillways. The gate blocking access was unlocked. Somehow, Charlie knew that it would be.

He pointed across the lake. "Normally, they come down the canyon and hover over the lake for a while." And pointing the other direction, "Sometimes, they come from downstream."

"So, what now?" Dennis asked.

"Now we wait."

*****

The waiting took hours and still no sign of any alien craft. It was foolhardy to think that they would just randomly see one on any given night. But Charlie knew. Just like knowing that the gate would be unlocked, Charlie knew that there would be one tonight.

"What were we thinking? This drunk doesn't know shit about any alien spaceship. We're just wasting our time."

"Yeah, let's get out of here."

Three of them started back towards the car.

"You guys coming?" they called over their shoulders.

"Nah, I'm staying."

"Me, too. It looks like Paul and me are both staying," yelled Dennis.

The three of them disappeared into the darkness, leaving Charlie with his two remaining companions. Paul let out a series of off-tune whistles, a poor attempt at recreating the X-Files theme.

Maybe ten minutes after the other three left sight, a stiff breeze blew up the canyon. A dark object glided up the Santa Ynez River towards the dam. As it came to the foot of the dam, it suddenly changed directions. Without a sound or any sign of slowing, it shot upwards until it crested the dam and hovered about twenty feet over their heads.

The craft was shaped like a Vienna sausage. A school bus sized Vienna sausage painted black with ugly red portholes along its length. A single light in its end flicked on, illuminating the top of the spillway.

Paul stood fixed, staring into the light. Dennis grabbed onto him, pulling him down the catwalk.

"We've got to get out of here. Paul! Snap out of it! Come on."

Paul followed Dennis. Slow and lethargic at first, but then looking over his shoulder, he started running. The two of them raced after their friends.

"Wait, you're missing it. Come back."

Charlie chased after them, waving. But Charlie was not in the athletic shape of his younger years and he quickly lost Paul and Dennis. Wheezing, he stopped next to his pick-up. He leaned against it, hoping to catch his breath.

*****

Dennis and Paul ran past the truck. Their friends had already left in the car, but their headlights could be seen just a little bit down the road.

"Let's cut through this way. The road turns back at the bottom of this hill." Dennis shouted, pointing down the chaparral covered hill.

The ground was slick and larger plants had been burnt away in a forest fire. With nothing to grab onto, the pair of them tumbled down the blackened hillside. They collapsed into an ignominious pile at the roadside. Dennis saw headlights coming down the road towards them. They had caught up with their friends.

Dennis sprang to his feet. Waving his arms as he ran towards the oncoming car.

"Hey, guys! Stop the car! Stop the car!"

The car rounded the corner, but only a single headlight illuminated the road. It moved towards Dennis without a sound. Dennis skidded on the gravel and spun around. He raced back to Paul and pulled him to his feet.

"Get up. It's not the guys. It's the aliens. We've got to get out of here."

Paul squealed in terror upon seeing the craft sliding through the air towards them. He sprang forward like a frightened deer. Dennis followed close behind. The pair left the road and raced down the hill. They slid down the hard scrabble of the canyon side, not stopping until they reached the river.

Dennis looked back up the hill. The beam of light traced the road above them. There was no sign that the UFO had seen them.

"Did we lose them?"

"I think so. But it's still up there. Let's hide out here for a while. Maybe until morning."

Dennis checked his phone. He had half a battery, but no bars. They couldn't call for help. But at least he could get a picture of the thing.

He fumbled with his phone trying to get the camera app. His thumb repeatedly smashed the icon in vain hope that it would make it open faster. As the camera app opened, Dennis pointed the back of the phone towards the alien craft moving above him on the road.

The pictures came back blurry. They ended looking like an out of focus black van.

"Damn it! Paul, check your phone. Why ain't I using video?"

Feeling like a fool, he switched the camera setting to video and started recording. This time, he did it with commentary.

"This is Dennis Hoffman. I'm standing next to the Santa Ynez River and you aren't going to believe what I just saw. What I'm showing you right now…"

"I've got bars."

"Well, then call someone, Paul!"

"Who?"

Dennis spun towards Paul, a huff escaping from his lips. His eyes and mouth wide with amazement at Paul's apparent stupidity.

"I don't know, the Air Force, the Police, even the Fire Department."

Paul dialed. Dennis could hear Paul's phone trying to connect. He turned back towards the hill. There was no sign of the aliens up on the road.

"Where did they go?"

"911, How may I direct... {crackle}"

"I got disconnected, Dennis."

Suddenly, a brilliance washed across the entire shoreline. Dennis shielded his eyes. The bright light felt warm against his skin. Silently, the alien craft hovered along the riverbank. The silence was deafening. Dennis screamed at Paul, but the sound refused to carry beyond his lips. Paul stood dumbfounded, staring into the blinding aura.

The light lasted but an instant and then darkness. Red glow from the portholes was the only evidence of the ship's presence.

A slice of yellow light appeared in the side of craft and a ramp extended down to the shore. A pair of short figures appeared in the opening and started moving down the ramp. The front alien lifted an oblong pistol, aimed at Dennis, and nothing happened. Whatever its purpose, Dennis was unaffected.

He reached down and grabbed a rock from the ground. Hearkening back to his high school baseball days, he pitched it straight at the armed alien, knocking it off the ramp into the water below. He knelt to grab a second stone, but his hands closed around a tree branch, instead.

Dennis jumped up and charged at the second alien just as it stepped onto the shore. He swung the piece of driftwood like a bat, hitting the alien in the face. He brought his club down on his foe's head, knocking it off its feet. Blue blood spurted from a large gash. Dennis shifted the branch in his hand to get a better grip.

As he swung on the prone target, the first alien sprinted up the shore and tackled him. The two of them tumbled to the ground. Dennis rolled on top of the alien and punched it in the face. The alien's resilience and wiry strength surprised him.

"Charlie! Charlie!" he shouted. "Where are you?"

*****

Charlie stumbled down the hill towards the screaming. Without a flashlight, the darkness loomed in on him and he tripped more than once on exposed roots and sandstone.

He half-ran, half-slid down to the river's edge. The alien craft hovered silently along the shore; a ramp extended to the ground. Light shone from the open portal, illuminating the people standing there.

Paul stood motionless, mouth agape, staring blankly into the night. Dennis wrestled with a small, gray alien. Another alien lay face down on the wet ground, blue blood trickling from a head wound.

The aliens' bald, egg-shaped heads and emaciated bodies and limbs matched with the pervasive description of "Greys". The larger man should have easily overpowered his smaller opponent, but the alien possessed a strength belied by its skinny stature.

Noticing Charlie, Dennis screamed, "Help me with this thing."

"On my way."

Charlie sprinted towards Dennis. Reaching into his jacket pocket, he pulled out his dad's old service revolver. Charlie didn't even remember bringing it with him. Holding it in his hand reassured him as he ran.

He skidded to a halt. Gravel and sand sprayed the wrestlers. He pointed his gun.

"Get off him!"

"Shoot him! Shoot him!"

"I was talking to you, Dennis."

Charlie didn't know where that came from. It came unbidden from his own lips. Dennis stared at him in horror.

Slowly, he cocked the hammer and pulled the trigger. The pistol hopped in his hand. Dennis jerked from the impact, falling away from the alien. Charlie kept pulling the trigger. Round after round slammed into Dennis's body.

The clack of the hammer against empty cartridges brought Charlie to his senses. He was screaming. He couldn't comprehend what he had just done nor why.

Glancing around, he saw a third alien tending to its unconscious companion. Dennis's assailant recovered itself and stood before Charlie. The alien's huge black eyes pierced through Charlie, making him shudder.

The Greys made high pitched chirps. Somehow, Charlie could understand them.

"Why was this one immune to our paralysis emitter?" said the close one, pointing at Dennis.

"I don't know," replied the new arrival. "We will take its body and perform an autopsy."

"What about our agent?" the first asked, staring back at Charlie. "He has brought us specimens so many times, it would be a shame to lose him."

"Send him back to his conveyance. He will forget this, just like the other times. His implants will ensure that. We will take care of the rest."

"Agreed," said the first, "It is so much easier to purge these computerized devices they use now. Remember when they used celluloid film? You couldn't remotely change files and their devices didn't transmit a signal to follow." Then something akin to a chuckle.

Both aliens stared at Charlie with their unblinking eyes.

"You may go."

Charlie stumbled away. Other times? He remembered his own abduction six years ago. He remembered seeing their ships other times. But he had never managed to convince anyone else to come up here with him. And what did the aliens mean by calling him "their agent".

His feet kept moving forward. Each step coming from a will not his own. The walk back to his truck seemed to take hours.

*****

Charlie jerked awake. Someone was banging on the side of the truck. Squinting through the brightness of the morning sun, he saw Bob Long, one of the local forest rangers, staring at him through the open window.

"Charlie, wake up. I've told you before you can't be up here. This road isn't for public access. Only Forest Service and people working on the dam can use it. Why don't you just drive home?"

"Okay, Bob. I'll do that. Sorry to bother you."

Charlie's sight began to clear. His head throbbed and his back hurt from another night sleeping in the cab of his pick-up.

"Do you know anything about that Camry parked in the bushes down the road?"

Charlie took in a breath to steady himself. His hangover was killing him. He didn't remember seeing any other cars on his way up here.

"Nope. Can't say I saw anyone else up here last night."

"Alright, I didn't see anyone around. I'll call it in once I get back down to the highway."

Charlie just nodded as he fumbled with his keys.

"And, Charlie, clean up your empties before you leave."

As Bob walked back to his own truck, Charlie climbed out of his truck to gather up the cans from last night's twelve pack. Another night wasted to alcohol and vague recollections of aliens from so long ago.

THE END

THE DEAD

Not everything dead is gone.

Not everything stays buried.

MOLL DYER'S REVENGE

by Mike Marcus

Frank poured a cup of dark, steaming coffee,
spooning sugar into the heavy ceramic mug. Above
him, rain drummed steadily on the roof. Today's plans
were shot, but retirement offered plenty of opportunity
for fishing. The rainswept Saturday was now dedicated
to a strong pot of coffee, a wool blanket, and the dog-
eared Stephen King paperback he picked up at the used
bookstore in town.

Hot coffee sloshed over his hand and across the
counter with the first bang on the front door.

"Frank! Frank! Are you home?"

He recognized his neighbor's voice but paused,
not ready to give up the quiet day he knew would be
lost if he answered. Frank wiped up the spill with a
damp washrag and leaned against the counter. Jim
Winthrop knew he was inside; he'd walked past

Frank's Jeep in the driveway to bang on the front door. It wasn't that Frank didn't like Jim; he just didn't have much in common with the forty-something computer programmer. Jim and his teenage daughter Sara were nice enough and generally quiet, keeping to themselves on the one-lane gravel road they shared with Frank. He joined them occasionally for cookouts and they had a good time. It was just that Frank didn't want neighbors, regardless how nice they were.

Frank hoped Jim would give up, but the banging grew more frantic. He swung open the heavy wooden door, rain from the uncovered front porch blowing inside. Jim still had his hand raised in a white-knuckled fist to pound and almost looked surprised that Frank had answered.

"Sorry, Jim, I didn't hear you knocking. I was in the john and thought it was thunder," Frank said, stepping back into the foyer and away from the blowing rain. It was only then Frank realized that Jim was soaked to the bone and completely oblivious to the downpour.

Tall and lanky, Jim swayed like a cornstalk about to topple. His cheeks were flushed and his eyes bloodshot.

"Thank god you're home. You used to be a cop, right? In Pittsburgh?" Jim asked, stepping into the house and closing the door behind him. Water dripped down his jeans, leaving muddy little pools around his tennis shoes. Frank saw the rain puddling on the floor and was glad he replaced the entryway carpet with linoleum last year.

Jim knew Frank had retired from the Pittsburgh police. They talked about it every time Jim invited him over. Sara always wanted to hear about the murder cases he worked while Jim encouraged Frank to talk about his time in Vice busting drug dealers. About a year ago, Jim confided in Frank that they moved from Jacksonville for a fresh start. Liz, Sara's mother, died when she was only seven and neither of them ever really recovered from the loss. Jim dove into work to distract himself after Liz died and never really reconnected with his daughter. Liz and Sara were a matched pair and when Liz died, Jim didn't know how to be a single parent. He worked too much and Sara got mixed up with the wrong kids in school. Just after she turned sixteen, she snuck out of the house and ended up in the hospital. Sara swore it was the first time she'd tried any drugs. Jim tried to believe her but had doubts; Frank knew better. Snorting heroin wasn't usually a kid's first experience with drugs.

Jim decided to move them somewhere free from their shared ghosts. A position with his company opened up at the Navy base in Southern Maryland not far from where he grew up in Leonardtown. The Winthrop family could be traced back to some of the first families in the area. They didn't have any immediate family left there, but he hoped returning to their roots would be a good start for them both.

"Sara's missing and the police won't help. I think she's been gone for at least two days," Jim said, running his hands through his wet hair.

"Are you sure she's missing? Could she just be out with friends and forgot to tell you?"

"I already checked. They don't know where she is. I just got back from the Sheriff's office, but they won't investigate a missing seventeen-year-old unless there's evidence something happened. I know she didn't run off. Something happened to my little girl and they won't help me," he said, collapsing onto the bench next to the door, his head in the hands.

Frank put a heavy hand on Jim's shoulder, letting the man weep. Comforting a victim's family was the part of the job Frank hated the most. It wasn't that he was cold hearted, but as a detective, Frank was a bloodhound. Let him loose on a trail and he'd run down the bad guy. Don't tie him up with emotions and personal issues. Find the clues, piece them together, and collar the crook. That's how Frank functioned.

He knew the Sheriff's office was correct, but it wasn't what Jim wanted to hear. Teenagers went missing every day and were usually found at friend's or relative's home. Nearly two years ago, Jim yanked Sara out of the only home she knew. The Sheriff's office figured she was either shacked up with a boyfriend or was on her way back to Jacksonville. It was the same determination he would have made. Despite this, Frank reached into the kitchen junk drawer for a pen and one of his old leather-bound notepads.

"Okay, let's start from the beginning. Tell me what happened."

*****

Frank pulled on his black raincoat and Steelers ballcap, tucking the notebook and pen into the inside pocket, exactly where he carried it when he was still on the force. The weight of the notebook against his chest felt good and Frank realized it was one of those little things he missed. He paused for a second at the door and thought about getting the shoulder holster from the closet. His .45 was in the safe beneath his bed. I'm not a cop anymore. I'm not even a private investigator. I'm just a neighbor helping out, he thought, leaving the holster and pistol.

Jim was asleep on the sofa and would be for some time thanks to one of Frank's little pink pills. Frank's doctor gave him a prescription for Ambien when he started having problems sleeping. The problem, though, wasn't sleeping; it was the victims still whispering to him as he tried to rest. The pills helped sometimes, but Frank didn't like the way he felt the next morning, so the prescription just grew outdated in the medicine cabinet.

The rain turned to a light drizzle as Frank walked down Black Fern Lane to the Winthrop house. The gravel crunched beneath his boots, cutting through the patter of rain on tree leaves. Jim and Sara's place was a couple hundred yards down the road and around the slight bend, a stand of maple trees blocking the view from Frank's kitchen window. Stepping onto the front porch, Frank reviewed his notes.

Five days ago, Jim flew to Atlanta for work. Sara was at school when he left but the night before they'd discussed the rules while he was gone – no boys and no parties. They'd gone grocery shopping that night. He took their only car to the airport. Jim texted Sara twice a day while he was gone, but she didn't always respond right away. The last message Jim received from Sara was Wednesday morning as she was getting ready for school. Since moving to Leonardtown, Jim travelled for work every few months and Sara stayed home by herself without any issues. She saw a counselor twice a month and had gotten involved at school. Jim thought she'd turned a corner from the problems in Jacksonville.

Jim returned home late the previous night but didn't realize Sara was missing until around 9 a.m. this morning. She was usually up before him on Saturdays, drinking coffee in the living room and either reading or texting with friends. Jim found her cell phone on her nightstand, his last three text messages to her unread, as well as a series of messages from her best friend, Anna Mowery. Frank circled this in his notebook. Teenagers didn't leave without their cell phone. That was the one thing they always took with them.

Jim searched the house this morning. Nothing was out of place or missing, other than his daughter. He found three days of mail and newspapers still in the mailbox. Sara was last seen at school on Wednesday, and there didn't appear to be any contact with her since then.

Frank wiped his boots on the doormat and stepped into the house. The living room was a lot like his own. Family photos sat on a long console table beneath a bay window that looked down into the dense woods behind the house. Television and stereo in their usual place. The carpet was clean. No signs of a party or a break-in.

Frank found Sara's room down a short hallway. He wished he'd grabbed latex gloves from his first aid kit. He didn't want to contaminate the crime scene, if it turned out that's what he discovered. The odds were still good that Sara would turn up, but he'd have to risk leaving his prints and DNA in the room. If something did happen to Sara, it was easy enough to explain that Jim asked him to investigate.

Frank found himself following the same procedures he used in his thirty-five years in uniform. Keep to the perimeter of the room. Don't touch anything unless absolutely necessary. Look for anything out of place – disturbed dust on shelves, tape where photos had been adhered to mirrors but were now missing, dresser drawers left open and rummaged through when the rest of the room was tidy.

Nothing looked out of place or missing, but that was always a challenge to determine in a teenager's room. Clothes scattered about, books stacked haphazardly, magazine photos taped to the walls, stuffed animals piled on an unmade bed. It was the typical teenage girl's room. He'd have Jim check Sara's clothes to see if any were missing, though he doubted the father would necessarily know.

Frank leaned over the open laptop on the cluttered desk and tapped the spacebar to dismiss the screen saver. Facebook, Twitter, and Instagram were bookmarked and each opened without problem, the passwords saved by the web browser. No posts or activity from Sara since Wednesday evening. Frank scrolled through her search history. Amtrak and Greyhound pages for tickets to Jacksonville. Jim wouldn't be happy to hear that, but at least it reinforced that she probably wasn't taken.

Next to the laptop was a legal pad with just a few yellow pages remaining. Frank took a dark crayon from a desk drawer and lightly ran it over the top page, revealing the writing from the pages that had been above it. Over and over again the name "Moll Dyer" appeared, sometimes in the flowery handwriting of a teenage girl, others times in large, heavy block letters. Frank snapped a picture with his phone to follow up. He stopped at the door and took one last look around the bedroom. If something happened to Sara, it didn't happen here.

Back in his own dining room, Frank called the St. Mary's County Sheriff's Department. A deputy answered on the third ring and Frank asked to be transferred to Captain Ben Henson.

Henson ran the department's Special Operations division, which was pretty much everything except Vice and Patrol. Henson's predecessor, Larry Fitzsimmons, introduced Frank and Ben. Fitzsimmons gave Frank the idea to move to Southern Maryland when he retired from the Pittsburgh Police. They'd met at a homicide investigation conference in Baltimore and after a few beers in the hotel bar realized they both had a passion for fishing. That summer Frank spent a week on the Potomac River, puttering around the little estuaries in a jon boat. That week, Larry introduced Ben and Frank over a bucket of beers at Two Knuckleheads, a bar where Frank and Ben still met up occasionally. After that week on the water, Frank decided that he'd retire to St. Mary's County.

After the requisite Saturday morning small talk, Frank explained that Jim Winthrop turned up at his door. Frank told Ben that he was pretty confidant she had either run away or was shacking up with a boyfriend her father didn't know about, but he just wanted to follow up with the Sheriff's Department.

Ben confirmed Frank's suspicions. That morning Jim Winthrop burst into the Sheriff's Department yelling that his daughter had been kidnapped and demanding they put out an Amber Alert. Ben and two deputies calmed him down enough to get the story but he was still a mess when he'd left. The deputies took the missing persons report and sent a copy to the Jacksonville PD in case they picked her up there. Jim wasn't too happy they wouldn't do more.

Frank shared with Ben what he'd found, and not found, at the Winthrop home that morning. Ben wasn't surprised. In rural counties like St. Mary's, Ben said, every few years a teenage girl disappeared. Sometimes they returned a day or two later with a bad hangover, sometimes they came home a few years later with a baby, and sometimes they never showed up again, but there was never any evidence of a kidnapping or foul play. Sometimes girls just disappear.

Hearing that Sara had shopped for bus tickets, Ben recommended Frank talk with Mary Calvin, the director of the county women's shelter. Most runaways in the county tended to show up at the shelter at some point, Ben said, especially because the shelter was known to give gift cards to women leaving bad situations, helping with bus tickets to a safe place. Security was tight at the shelter and Ben offered to call ahead and let Mary know Frank would be coming. He gave Frank the address just outside of Leonardtown and promised to buy the first bucket of beers at Two Knuckleheads if the case turned out to be more than just a runaway teenager.

*****

The county women's shelter was a large three-story colonial home on a short dead-end street. A wrought-iron fence surrounded the property with security cameras on light posts. Frank pressed the button on the telecom at the gate and asked for Mary Calvin, holding up his retired police credentials to the camera. He was buzzed through and greeted by a receptionist just inside the double-front doors, where she checked his ID, asked if he was armed, and escorted Frank down a narrow hallway to Mary Calvin's office. Ancient sepia-toned photos of Leonardtown lined the pale yellow walls.

"Good morning, Mr. Connelly. What can I do for you this morning?" Mary Calvin asked as she entered the office from a side door.

Frank was surprised. He expected an older, more matronly director and not the forty-something, very attractive woman standing before him.

Mary was tiny but solid. She just cleared five feet tall but she was all business. Her dark, curly hair was up in a ponytail, and her plain grey t-shirt and faded blue jeans, covered in splatters of dried paint and bleach splotches, had the look of a women who was hands-on in her work. Her confidence screamed she would never find herself in a position she couldn't handle.

"These are great photos of the town. I don't think I've seen any going this far back, not even in the town library," Frank said.

"I have a particular interest in the town's history. I can trace my roots here back to the mid-1700s," Mary told him. Her deep blue eyes, sparkling a moment before, darkened with a look of concern. "But I don't think you're here for a history lesson."

"No, I'm sorry. Ben Henson recommended I come speak with you. I'm looking for Sara Winthrop, a local girl we believe is a runaway. Ben said a lot of girls make their way through here looking for help."

"I'm sorry, but I can't tell you if she is or has been here. We are a refuge of last resort for many women, and they trust us to keep them safe," the director said. "You aren't related to the girl, are you?"

"No, ma'am. I'm retired Pittsburgh police. The girl's father asked me this morning to help look for her when he discovered she was missing. I live down the street from them," Frank explained, handing his retired police identification card to her. "I understand your need to protect your clients' privacy, but this is a seventeen-year-old girl with a drug history. Name is Sara Winthrop. Blond hair, blue eyes, about 5'6", 125 pounds. Her father came home last night from a business trip and realized this morning that she was missing. We think she disappeared sometime Wednesday evening or maybe Thursday morning."

Mary handed the black leather ID holder back to Frank, reopening the hallway door back to the entrance. "I'm sorry, Mr. Connelly. Knowing that, I can tell you that Sara hasn't been here. We haven't had anyone here recently with that name or who fits that description."

"Thank you, Ms. Calvin. If Sara does show up, please let her know that her dad just wants to make sure she's safe. He wants to know she's okay."

"I doubt Sara will show up here," Mary said, walking Frank back the front doors. "I think you know as well as I do, if this girl ran away, there was a reason and she's probably not coming back."

*****

Frank sat at the kitchen table and checked his notes, his neighbor still snoring on the couch. Jim said he'd called Anna Mowery, Sara's best friend, but Frank wanted to follow up. He called the number Jim had given him. He introduced himself and Anna said she'd been expecting his call, that Sara's father told her earlier that morning that he was asking a friend to help find her. Glad he started throwing my name around before he bothered to ask me to help, Frank thought, but immediately slipped into the usual missing persons questions.

Anna confirmed she last spoken with Sara on Wednesday at school. They texted a few times that evening, and Anna sent messages again Thursday and Friday when Sara didn't show up for class. Anna said she didn't know of any plans Sara had to run away. Teen girls may be experts at hiding things from their parents, but kept few secrets from their best friend. Maybe Sara's bus ticket research didn't mean anything after all. Frank was wrapping up when he thought of the legal pad next to the laptop and asked Anna if Moll Dyer was a classmate he should speak with.

"No," Anna said with a laugh. "You aren't from around here, are you? It's a legend we all learn growing up here. A couple hundred years ago there was this witch, Moll Dyer. She lived in the woods outside of town. One winter, they burned her house down and she froze to death in the woods. There's a big rock in front of the courthouse that she supposedly died on. They say you can see her hand and knee prints in the rock, but it just looks like a rock to me. What does she have to do with Sara?"

"Probably nothing," Frank said. "Thanks for your help. If you think of anything else, let me know."

*****

Frank opened his laptop and typed "Moll Dyer" into his search engine. A handful of Maryland legend websites popped up. Frank read through several, each with their own slight differences, though the main story appeared to be pretty consistent.

Moll Dyer, an Irish immigrant, lived in Leonardtown in the late 1600s. Dyer was the town midwife, described as an old hag, rounded of back and long of tooth with stringy grey hair. She lived in a cottage in the woods outside of town with a large white dog or wolf, depending on who told the story.

In 1697, a particularly harsh snowstorm hit the county, killing cattle and sheep in the fields. This was only a few years after the Salem witch trials, and several town residents accused the old woman of witchcraft. Men from the town burned her cottage, believing she was inside, but several days later she was found in the woods, her frozen body stretched across a large rock.

According to legend, she cursed the land around her cottage. When the forest was cleared and turned to farmland, it refused to bear any crops and eventually returned to wild woodland.

In the 1970s, town officials moved the rock on which she was supposedly found to its current location outside the county courthouse in Leonardtown. Moll Dyer Road and Moll Dyer's Run, located just outside of town supposedly passed by where her cottage once stood. Occasionally, locals – usually after a few drinks – still report sightings of strange, human-shaped mists, unnatural lights and white wolves.

A map on one website showed the location of Moll Dyer Road, Moll Dyer's Run, and other nearby roads, including Black Fern Lane. The Winthrop house was only about a mile through the woods from Moll Dyer Road, and Sara's bedroom window faced the woods where Moll Dyer's cottage once supposedly stood.

Frank knew Sara Winthrop was most likely on a bus headed to Jacksonville, but something just didn't sit well with him. One of his former partners once said that Frank's gut had more brains than his head and he'd learned early on as a detective not to ignore his intuition. Something told him this wasn't just another run away, but he didn't have anything to give to the Sheriff's office except a gut feeling.

Frank picked up his phone and called Ben Henson.

"Somehow, I knew you'd be calling me, but I guess it's not about buying me lunch, is it? Any luck with the missing Winthrop girl?" Ben asked.

"I may be on a wild goose chase, but have you had any reports of strange lights back in the woods down the hill from Black Fern Lane?"

Frank heard Ben chuckle through the phone. "You mean down off Moll Dyer Road?"

"Yeah. Sara was reading about the Moll Dyer legend. I'm starting to wonder if maybe she went looking for the cottage and got lost in the woods."

"Or did Moll Dyer kidnap Sara Winthrop?" Ben joked. "Every few years we get a hunter reporting lights in the woods, sometimes even the ghostly figure of a woman. Maybe once a year someone says they saw a big white dog crossing the road, but it's nothing. There's a lot of swamp around here and we get fog in the woods."

"Even so, what would it take to get a couple of officers to do a sweep of the woods between the Winthrop house and Moll Dyer Road? Just in case?"

"Sorry, buddy. Not a chance. We don't have the resources to put toward a search of an area that big – that's almost 500 acres of woods and swamp. Unless you've got something more than a hunch, there's no way I can get the Sherriff on board and even then, we'd probably need state police support."

"I figured but I had to ask. Have they ever found exactly where Moll Dyer's house was? If Sara went looking for it, at least I'd know what direction to look."

"Supposedly it was somewhere back on Moll Dyer Road, but I don't know exactly. If you really want to chase down this idea, you should talk to Grandma Mabel. She lives in an old mobile home right where Moll Dyer Road meets Route 5. If there's anyone who knows, it'd be her. Do me a favor, though. Don't go out there and get lost in the woods. I can guarantee we won't be sending anyone out looking for you. Also, there's a few things you should know about Grandma Mabel before you go out there."

*****

Frank pulled his Jeep off the highway onto the muddy path of Moll Dyer Road. Heavy tree branches blocked out the cloudy sky creating a dark tunnel through the woods. Off to the right sat an ancient mobile home with a sagging porch of rough-cut timber. An old woman who could have been no one but Grandma Mabel sat in a porch swing, gently rocking and petting a black cat perched on her lap. Frank parked on a patch of crushed oyster shells next to the trailer and took the paper grocery bag from the passenger seat.

"Watchoo want, boy?" the woman called as Frank approached. Ben said she may be the oldest person in the county but Frank was still surprised by her obvious age. Her face was a map of wrinkles and deep creases. She turned to follow Frank as he approached but her eyes were milky with heavy cataracts covering her pupils, making Frank wonder if she could see or was just following the sound of his footsteps. Her nose was long and thick, her cheeks narrow and gaunt. She wore a long-sleeved flannel nightgown and cheap slippers, only her bony calves and feet exposed. Another black cat wound its way around her feet while a third perched on the nearby windowsill.

"Ma'am. My name is Frank Connelly. I live down on Black Fern Lane and I'm looking for a girl who's gone missing. Ben Henson said I should come talk to you. I need to know about Moll Dyer and where her house may have stood," Frank said.

"Whatchoo bring me? Ben didn't send you emptyhanded. He made that mistake himself years ago, yes he did," she said with a sudden widemouthed cackle, revealing pink toothless gums. The hair on Franks arms and neck stood on end.

"Yes ma'am. Here you go," Frank said, setting the bag at her feet. He'd stopped at the market and picked up the strange assortment of items Ben recommended. A quart of fresh oysters, a box of white candles, a pack of Marlboro reds, a six-pack of Budweiser, a fifth of cinnamon whiskey, and three MoonPies.

"Good, good. You ain't from 'round here. Why you botherin' Moll, askin' all 'bout her?"

"I think the lost girl may have gone into the woods to find where her house was supposed to have been, or maybe where she died. I saw the rock in front of the courthouse…"

"That rock ain't nuthin' but a stone somebody found back in the woods," she said, staring at Frank with blind eyes and chomping her toothless gums. A pink tongue slithered from the corner of her mouth and wet her lips. "I like you boy. You got a good face, even if you ain't from 'round here. Sit down there. I'm gonna tell you the truth 'bout Moll. First thing you gotta wrap your head round is Moll Dyer ain't dead. She ain't never been dead, and I don't think she ever gonna be dead. Rage like that don't ever die. When Moll and her daughter left Cuba…"

"Wait, I thought she came from Ireland. And I didn't know she had a daughter," Frank interrupted.

"If you wanna hear the story, you need to shut yo' mouth and let me tell it. No more interruptions or we're done and you can just be on your way."

"Yes ma'am."

"As I was sayin', Moll and her daughter, Alannah, were in Cuba, workin' on a sugarcane plantation for a few years before comin' to the county. Back in Ireland she was a midwife, but in Cuba her girl came down sick and Moll couldn't do nothin' to save her. It was the women down there saved Alannah, and Moll learned their magic before they came here."

"Moll and Alannah settled in an old hut back in the woods, just yonder," she continued, pointing one knobby, arthritic hand over the nearby rise in the woods. "They tended the village, birthin' babes, curing the sick, but always keepin' to themselves. The men knew Moll and Alannah practiced the arts, but they let them be as long as they didn't hurt no one. But then one of the boys fell in love with Alannah. Love don't bring nothin' but pain, you best know that. Them two knew they couldn't marry. A proper family like that can't have no witch as a daughter. Things went bad when a travellin' preacher came through. Some other girl jealous of Alannah told that there were witches livin' here."

"That night they came for Moll and Alannah. The men thought they caught them in their hut and set it to fire, but Moll was out collecting wood. Moll watched from the trees, listening to her daughter's screams as she was burnt alive. The girl was only seventeen."

"Them legends you read got it right in one way. Moll cursed the lands 'round here that night. Nothin's ever grown here but trees and vines. I can't grow no tomatoes or nothin' without them witherin'. Moll hid in the woods 'til the men were gone, kept warm by that wolf Alannah raised from a pup. She swore that night that she'd take their daughters, just like they took hers, and she's been doin' just that ever since. Every few years a girl disappears. The police just say they run off, but I know better. It's Moll takin' her revenge."

Grandma Mabel reached into the bag the Frank brought and pulled out a can of Budweiser, taking a long drink. Thin streams of beer slipped from the upturned corners of her mouth and ran down her neck, disappearing beneath the nightgown's tatty ruffled collar.

"How is it the legend that everyone tells is so different?" Frank asked after she finished the beer with a smack of her lips.

"Whatchoo think? It's easier to accept a witch died in the cold than that your ancestors burned two women alive."

What if the legend everyone knew really was the sanitized version, one that didn't sound quite as bad as the one Grandma Mabel just told, Frank thought. "Where did you hear this version of the legend?"

The old woman let loose another cackle and lifted the quart of raw oysters from the bag, pulling off the plastic top and dipping two clawed fingers inside, scooping out one of the dripping oysters and sucking it between her toothless gums. "It's gettin' dark. You best be getting' home. You don't wanna get lost out in 'dem woods at night," she warned with a broad smile, picking up the bag and disappearing into the darkness inside the trailer.

*****

Frank sat with Jim and reviewed most of what he'd learned. He left out everything about Moll Dyer, unsure how to even explain the legend, much less Grandma Mabel. The odds were still best that Sara was on her way to Jacksonville, and hopefully the local PD or a family friend would find her before she got into too much trouble. With that hope, Frank sent Jim home to contact any old friends in Jacksonville to keep an eye out for her. As darkness settled in, Frank opened the bottle of cinnamon whiskey he bought for himself.

The next morning, Frank rode over to the Army/Navy surplus in Lexington Park, picking up a ruck sack, compass, and a better flashlight, as well as new boots. With a topographical map of the county, Frank started daily hikes through the woods, covering the area between Black Fern Lane and Moll Dyer Road, looking for any sign of Sara. After almost a week, he'd covered most of the direct routes from the Winthrop house without any sign of the girl. Every other day he stopped in to check on Jim, who was still optimistic Sara would show up in Jacksonville. He'd been in contact with everyone they knew down there and he was thinking of taking a trip down there to look for her himself. Frank never mentioned his hikes through the woods.

Ten days. Sara was missing for ten days when Frank accepted that searching the woods wasn't going to pay off. The next morning would be his last hike, retracing his steps one more time, hoping he'd missing some sign that Sara had been there. Frank stood on his front porch and watched the moon rise through the trees, a glass of cinnamon whiskey on the porch railing

111

and a stubby cigar clenched between his teeth. He was well into his cigar when he saw the movement. Moonlight trickled through the leaves in tiny patterns of dancing light as the nighttime breeze off the Potomac River made the trees sway and shift in the darkness. Frank stepped off of the porch and saw a white wolf standing in the gravel road looking back at him. It disappeared into the brush at the edge of the lane, reappearing just into the woods heading behind the Winthrop house. It stopped and looked right at him.

"I've got to be fucking crazy," Frank said to himself, grabbing a flashlight from just inside the door and jogging toward where he last saw the creature. "I think a girl disappears in the woods searching for a dead witch and now I'm following a ghost wolf into the same woods."

Frank shone the flashlight where wolf had stood but saw nothing except swaying underbrush and faint fog beginning to form along the ground. He turned off the flashlight, his eyes adjusting to the darkness. The wolf stood just where he'd been looking a moment before with the flashlight. It started away at a slow trot, stopping repeatedly to glance back at Frank as though to ensure he was following. The further into the woods they moved, the thicker the fog grew until he crossed a small stream. It was Moll Dyer's Run, the creek that wound its way through the woods and paralleled the similarly named road. He'd crisscrossed the creek repeatedly over the last week but couldn't recall the clearing in which he now stood.

At the center stood a small cabin, moss and ferns growing on the roof. A stone chimney leaned precariously at one end, faint wisps of white smoke rising from the top. Fire light flickered through gaps in the shutters. Creeping low to the ground, Frank approached the cabin wishing he'd grabbed his .45 or at least his cell phone before heading into the woods. Nearing the cabin, he heard the crackling and popping of a fire and the faint sound of a woman singing. It was an old tune, likely Irish from the woman's accent. Frank knelt beneath the closed window for a second to catch his breath and then rose up, peering through the cracks in the shutter.

She couldn't have looked more like a witch if a Hollywood makeup team created her. Short and hunched, leaning heavily on a walking stick taller than she was, she tended a cauldron hanging in the hearth with her back to the window. Her long black cloak seemed to move and shift around her, as though it was made not of cloth but of the pure darkness of night. As she turned in the firelight toward a small stand with an aged silver mirror atop it, Frank caught a glimpse of her face. Grey sagging skin, a long, hooked nose. Knots of dirty grey hair filled with leaves and sticks hung down over her shoulders and around her face. Her hands were long and thin with bony, daggerlike fingers tipped with jagged fingernails stained black.

Frank nearly screamed when a soul wrenching howl pierced the quiet of the night, echoing through the woods over and over again until it sounded like a pack of direwolves surrounded the clearing. The witch chittered to herself inside the cabin and Frank peered through the shutter as she dished up a bowl from the cauldron and scuttled her way outside through another door. She set the bowl down in the clearing and the white wolf appeared at her side, lowering its snout. Frank could hear it eating voraciously, biting and licking at the contents of the bowl as the witch stroked its fur and cooed to it as if it were a child.

Frank slipped through the door on his side of the cabin, trying to absorb every detail of the clutter that filled the single room. From the rafters hung bunches of drying plants and flowers. Ceramic containers were scattered around the tables. On the shelves next to the mirrored stand were perfect rows of small, lidded ceramic crocks, each with a label attached by a thin black thread and a name written on each label in a fine, bloodred ink. With each container was a small item. A silver chain with a rainbow pendant. A red plastic hair barrette. A high school ring with a blue stone. Over and over, small personal items attached to a name and a small ceramic crock. Frank checked the window and saw the witch was still petting the wolf, it now licking her face like a puppy.

On the mirrored stand was another crock. "Sara Winthrop" was written on the label and with it sat a silver Claddagh ring with a green stone at its center. The ring belonged to Sara's mother, and Sara said she never removed it, not since her mother died. She'd shown it to Frank during one of the cookouts.

Frank heard the crack of a twig from outside and slipped back out the door just as the witch returned to the cabin. He watched through the crack in the shutter as she stood before the fire and shed the black cloak. Her body was sickly and thin, sores covering her sides and legs weeping a bloody yellow pus. Her skin was grimy and hung loose like an ill-fitting second-hand suit. She leaned heavily on the walking stick as she stepped to the mirrored stand, her flat, sagging breasts swaying with each wobbling step. She collapsed onto the small bench and stared up into the mirror where Frank could see her face clearly for the first time. Beneath the age and rot were piercing blue eyes as clear as a cloudless midday sky.

With one withered hand she lifted the lid from the crock with Sara's name and smeared her fingers with the yellow, waxy contents. She spread it over her arms and legs, returning to the crock over and over again for more until she'd coated her entire body with the greasy substance. Finally, scraping the last of it from the crock and filling her palms, she smeared it across her face, breathing deeply as she applied it like disgusting makeup. Frank watched as she stood, now without the aid of the walking stick, rising taller, stronger than she had been just minutes ago. As the firelight danced over her naked body, her skin tightened and grew healthy, the sores healing and disappearing. Her long, grey snarled hair shortened and darkened, curls forming in its length. Her breasts filled and rose firm, tipped with rosy, youthful nipples that perked in the cold breeze blowing through the cabin. She continued to grow younger and stronger, her skin pink and glowing in the firelight, until she leaned into the mirror to see herself. In the reflection was the face of Mary Calvin.

Frank dashed back into the woods in the direction from whence he came, hoping he could find his way back to the house. He flicked on his flashlight but after a few sputtering flashes, it died, leaving him

117

with only the glowing fog and fractured splinters of moonlight breaking through the branches. After what felt like hours, Frank stepped from the trees and found himself facing Grandma Mabel's trailer. The old woman sat in the darkness, gently rocking, a small kerosene lamp at her feet.

"Come on, boy. I know you out there. Come over and let's have us a talk."

Frank stumbled across the clearing, shaken by what he had seen.

"You done seen her, didn't you?" Grandma Mabel asked with a laugh. "She must've taken a shine to you if she let you in on her little secret. You probably got more questions now than before, don't you?"

"That…that was real? That was Moll Dyer. She is alive. She…she…"

"She alive, alright. Just as alive as you is. That was no legend I told you. That was the god's honest truth. You didn't believe me before but I think you believe me now."

"But Mary…Moll…she runs the women's shelter. If she is trying to help women, why is she killing them? Why is she using them to keep herself alive?"

"I'm not, not exactly," came Mary's voice from the darkness but with a newfound Irish lilt. From the shadows she stepped into the moonlight, wearing the same t-shirt and faded jeans as when Frank met her at the shelter. The wolf stepped out of the darkness behind her and sat in the grass.

"You're killing girls. I saw you use that stuff with Sara's name on it grow younger, to change from that old hag into this…this… form," Frank said, gesturing toward Mary. "And I saw the containers with the other girls' names. There had to dozens of them."

"More like 187, but who's counting? I'm simply collecting on a debt. I gave up my soul to save my daughter's life when she was sick, and then this town took her from me. I cursed each and every one of those men and swore I would not rest until I returned my pain upon them 1,000 times over. Every night I close my eyes and I see their faces in the firelight as they burned my child alive. Every night I repeat their names over and over and over again. Burgis. Cooksey. Lumpkins. Miles. Buckler. Winthrop. Their names are burnt into my memory. I will take their daughters as payment for what is owed to me and I'm not close to being done yet."

"So why run a women's shelter if you are going to kill their daughters? I don't understand."

"The shelter makes it all just so much sweeter. It lets me protect the other women who men always turned against. The weak, the helpless, the abused. What better way to bring my vengeance upon the men of this town than to take the daughters they love, and at the same time make their wives and other daughters strong and independent?"

"Why are you telling me this? You know there's nothing I can do to stop you, nothing I can do to stop any of this."

"Because I like you, Frank. I knew right away when we met that you've never hurt a woman, and in your eyes, I saw all of the women you helped before. Plus - you never know when a women's shelter could use the help of a retired police officer, now do you?" she said with a wry smile, turning and walking back into the woods.

"Wait! What am I supposed to tell Sara's father?"

"Tell him his daughter is dead and gone, never to return. Let me enjoy his tears and anguish," she said, disappearing into the misty darkness, the wolf at her heels.

Frank stood dumbfounded and started walking down the dirt road toward the highway and back home, unsure of how to come to terms with what he discovered. He hoped he'd wake up in the morning with a pounding headache from the cinnamon whiskey and realize this was all a bad dream, but he knew that wouldn't be the case.

"Boy, hey, boy," Grandma Mabel yelled out to him as he reached the end of the driveway. "I like you. Unless you want to get yo'self locked up, you best just keep this to yo' self. If 'dey don't believe me when I tell them about Moll, what makes you think any of 'dem going to believe you. You come back and see me tomorrow, and we talk some more. I got other stories you need to hear."

SPECTER HILL

by K.N. JOHNSON

Specters. Spook lights. Will-o'-the-wisps.
Locals found many names for the unusual lights
lurking in the woodlands of Clay County, but they
hadn't actually found out what was causing them.
When legends about the lights outnumbered Main
Street's potholes, engineers from the state university
came to investigate. Swamp gas. Fox fire. Elm tree
stumps. They measured, and they reasoned, offered a
theory even they deemed inconclusive. And that's why
Buck Bodean agreed to take a couple of legend-
trippers to Specter Hill.

"I know the backroads," Buck said, so
he took the lead with his truck kicking dust that clung
to the glossy black paint of their SUV. "Most folks
take Highway 40," he'd explained before they left
Kay's Café, "but we don't need the locals breathing
down our necks."

They parked in a scattering of gravel, a worn spot at the edge of the woods where others had once done the same. Where others, too, had waited for nightfall in search of the spectral lights. Here, daylight didn't depart of its own accord – it was consumed by a darkness that grew in the thick of the trees and poured over these strange hills just north of State Road 59.

Kevin tapped on Buck's window. The young man looked like a burro with a camera and tripod slung over each shoulder, a rucksack sagging down his back. His wife Valerie – or had he said girlfriend? – stood several feet behind him spraying every exposed bit of her skin with bug repellent.

Buck slid a fresh battery into his night vision camera and tightened the lid on his oversized travel cup. These two could be real die-hards. With their fancy equipment, they may want to search until dawn. Trekking through brambles on a humid Indiana night, though, had a way of sucking all the curiosity from a person, leaving them to wander not for wonders, but just a way out.

Valerie sprayed Kevin's calves and he jumped. "Look out for the gear, babe."

She tucked the can into his rucksack and held her mobile phone in the air. "No signal out here, huh?"

Buck slammed his truck door. "That's how folks get lost."

A shrine of sorts adorned the trailhead. A pair of tennis shoes, the laces tied together, hung from the branch of a tree, melted candles lined a fallen log. Buck placed a camping lantern on a lone rotted fence post and turned it on.

"Why's it red?" Valerie stooped extra low to avoid the dangling shoes.

"Specter Hill lights show up white, sometimes green." Buck lumbered up the trail with the beam of a penlight. "If we look for the red, we're sure to find our way back."

"It also signals that we're here." Kevin peered over his shoulder at the road, their vehicles. "Is that a good thing?"

Buck shrugged. "It's mostly just kids that come out here. No danger to us."

They followed the trail up the first hillside, down a valley, and around the second hill into the early morning hours. Once, Valerie insisted she'd seen a flashing light, but upon investigation, they all chuckled that she'd found a lightning bug. Kevin let out yet another bear of a yawn, so they decided to head back. Buck led them down the original hillside and there, through the thick bushes and leaves of the trees, they could all see the red lantern waiting for them.

*****

"Did you tell them?" Kay refilled Buck's coffee and leaned on the edge of the diner booth.

"Tell them what?" Buck stirred sugar into his black coffee.

"About your boy."

Buck looked out the café window. "Didn't seem necessary."

*****

This time, Kevin and Valerie showed up wearing cargo pants to cover their scratched legs. Buck nodded at the closed pail in Valerie's hand. "You planning on picking berries?"

Valerie pried the lid. "It's hay to lure the farmer's cow."

Buck scratched his chin. He'd told them a few of the tales, but they seemed most excited about the farmer and his wife. The farmer once owned a small farm on the other side of Specter Hill and one evening, his milk cow found a break in the fence and ran free. Wandered right into the woods. Well, the farmer's wife worried the cow would twist an ankle or, worse, fall into one of the old coal mining shafts hiding in these hills. Story goes, they each grabbed a lantern and started roaming the hill, calling for the cow over and over. No one knows if they ever found the cow because they never showed up at their farm again. Some say the spook lights are the farmer and his wife searching for their cow, their lanterns bouncing through the woods, night after night, for eternity.

"Let me say it this way." Buck cleared his throat. "You understand the cow would be dead by now, right?"

Kevin and Valerie both laughed. Her smile lifted one corner of her lips higher than the other. "It's a trigger object. Something that would have been special to the spirit when they were alive. We don't know anything about the farmer and his wife, but maybe if we bring the cow's spirit, we'll bring them, too."

These two are definitely die-hards, Buck thought.

Short of midnight, they reached the valley. The little box in Valerie's hand started blinking and she announced they should try to contact the spirits. She piled some of the hay on the lid of the pail as Kevin angled his cameras. Buck rolled a dead log closer and pointed his faint penlight at the pile.

Valerie called out, "Is there anyone here who wants to speak with us?"

An owl hooted, its *who-who* echoing the question into the trees.

Valerie held her mobile phone in front of one of the cameras. "I'm going to play some cow sounds." She pressed a button, cutting through the chirps and croaks of crickets and frogs with the long, plaintive moos of a cow.

Buck covered his mouth, afraid he'd chuckle, but the longer that cow cried into the night, the heavier his heart grew, the more intense his focus on that pile of hay.

"I'm shutting off the cow sounds." Valerie crouched beneath one of the cameras. Kevin knelt beside her.

The three listened. The owl had stopped hooting and even the crickets and frogs sounded farther away.

Valerie whispered. "Did you hear that?"

Buck cupped his ear. A breeze rustled the leaves above, parted the ferns below. The pile of hay rustled. It smelled more dusty than sweet, old and no longer fresh.

Valerie pointed at the pile, and Kevin nodded as he checked the preview on the back of the camera.

Buck crossed his arms. If these two were counting the wind as a spirit, they could've camped on one of the windmill farms and saved him the trouble. He stretched his legs and leaned back on the log when something tickled his ear. Valerie called out to the spirits again, but he didn't make out what she said, since he was busy swatting at what seemed to be nothing next to his ear. He ran his hand through his bushy hair, checking for a spider, and the sensation changed. The tickle disintegrated into an icy prickle and before he could rub away the cold, a woman's voice pressed close and uttered, "Bessie?"

Buck startled. His arms flew up and the log rolled from beneath him. As he landed on the ground, his legs kicked forward, pitching the pile of hay. He scrambled to his feet, frowning into the woods.

"She's here." Valerie hopped over the mess and darted past Buck, her arm stretched out with the little black box in hand. "Over here." She waved to Kevin who grabbed one of the cameras, tripod and all, and raced after her.

"Hey," Buck tried to raise his voice. "You've got to stay on the trail." He crawled through the underbrush looking for his penlight. He'd warned them. Told them the hills were filled with trouble spots that could break your neck. But here they went, running off after that voice. His fingers found the pen. He rubbed his ear. *Bessie.* Sounded like a cow's name. Could it really have been the farmer's wife?

He stepped from the trail, checking over his shoulder for the tiny red light on Kevin's other camera, and located them soon enough by the sound of a yelp and Valerie repeating, "I'm fine."

She clutched her knee, pulling her hands away at intervals to reveal a rip in her pants, a gash in her skin. Buck swept the penlight to the left where a broken gravestone jutted from the forest floor. He sighed. "Now, was that worth it?"

Valerie yanked on Kevin's hand to stand and smiled. "You bet it was. We hit the jackpot."

*****

Kay refilled each coffee cup and slid into the diner booth next to Buck. "You say you got pictures?"

Kevin thumbed some buttons on his video camera and held it so Buck and Kay could view the screen. It focused on a small pile of hay, pulled back until Buck's legs appeared on the side of the frame. Valerie's voice floated off camera, "I'm shutting off the cow sounds."

Buck held his hand in front of the screen and grumbled, "You can fast forward through this part."

Kevin rolled his eyes and fast forwarded. On screen, the dark woods jostled, the back of Valerie's shirt glowed a soft blue-gray until she came into focus. She pointed and the camera repositioned past her, past a large tree trunk until a light, a white orb, materialized. It levitated, yards ahead, rocking left to right.

"Well, I'll be." Kay nudged Buck's shoulder.

"And I recorded this, too." Valerie placed her mobile phone on the table and pressed Play.

A voice whispered from the speaker, "Bessie? Bessie?"

Buck shivered and leaned back in the seat.

Kay grinned. "You okay?" She patted his knee. "You look like you've seen a ghost."

Valerie glanced at Kevin, then tapped her phone. "There's no doubt he heard one."

*****

Buck hesitated in his truck. Kevin and Valerie stood by the fence post, weighed down with their usual gear. They'd convinced him to drive out for one more night. "It isn't phosphorous gas," they'd proclaimed that morning in the diner. "It's a haunting. A real haunting." They had debated whether Bessie was the name of the farmer's cow, whether it could be the name of another soul lost on Specter Hill. They asked him, "Has anyone else gone missing since the farmer and his wife?"

By then, Kay had left their table to serve another customer, and Buck was left to face their questions alone. He had grimaced and answered, "Yes."

They could barely contain themselves, leaning over the table with the expectation he would elaborate, but he pressed his lips together until he finally blurted that Bessie was, indeed, the most common name for a cow.

They hadn't pressed the matter, yet here he sat again. He'd been thinking about that hay, about that woman's voice in his ear. He'd been thinking about his boy. So, this time, Buck strode to the trailhead with an object in his own pocket. Something of his own choosing: an old baseball from his son's dresser. The treasured baseball from the only professional game his boy had attended.

They ambled to the valley of the previous night's activity and Valerie assembled a fresh pail of hay. She and Kevin unfolded a pair of camp chairs and situated themselves behind the cameras. Buck rolled the dead log into the shadows and settled onto the flattened greenery.

Valerie played the audio of the moaning cow. *Moo-moo.*

Buck tucked his hand in his pocket, ran his fingers over the threaded seams of the baseball. He allowed himself to remember his son's last words. "Everybody chases the lights at least once, Dad." He closed his eyes, pictured his son's tattered baseball cap, the leather mitt too big for his left hand, but he wore it everywhere anyway. His wife used to complain. "He's like that cartoon boy dragging that blue baby blanket around." And Buck had snapped,

"Years of difference between a blanket and a baseball mitt. Let him be."

Moo-ooo. Valerie announced for the camera she was shutting off the cow.

Buck clutched the baseball. He gripped it so tight, his fingers went numb.

Wind whirled down the hill, curled at their backs. A stick of hay trembled in the pile.

"Dad."

Buck jumped to his feet and stared at Kevin and Valerie as they, too, stood. They looked at each other, their eyes wide and mouths open.

"Da-ad."

Before Kevin could collect his camera equipment, Buck bolted from the trail. He flailed at branches. The penlight's beam flitted across his path until he found the neglected cemetery. He slowed, stepped over the broken and buried gravestones and paused where the woods escalated up the next hill.

"Dad." His son's voice beckoned.

He turned, the trail long behind him, and squinted. A light. A beacon bobbing ahead. He threw his body up the slope, grabbing small trees as his shoes lost traction. Higher and higher he climbed to a flat ridge. He bent, hands on his knees, and gasped for breath, the air now dank with mold.

"Da-ad."

Behind his legs, a light flickered. Buck stood and spun, his foot slipping on the damp rock. He grasped for leverage, leaned into the hill to avoid tumbling down, only to discover he was falling backward. Falling into the hill through a hole he hadn't seen. The steep shaft of rock scraped at his face and hands as he dropped into sheer darkness and landed with a thump.

Buck reached for his penlight. He gritted his teeth with pain, struggled to pull up on his elbows. The light flickered across the walls of a cave, the ceiling and hole far from reach. Buck groaned. He'd fallen down an abandoned coal shaft. He howled until he choked on his pleas and passed out from exhaustion.

Bright light flashed against his eyelids. Buck woke, held a hand in front of his face, hoped the night had duped him and here was the morning sun to berate his foolishness. He tried to sit but the light waned, rolled away. His penlight taunted him, casting a narrow beam into the dark cave.

He pulled his body, dragged his useless legs across the ground, aiming for the meager light. As he inched forward, something jabbed at his ribs. He reached underneath and pulled out, not a rock, but a cracked leather baseball mitt. He fumbled for the penlight, its beam softer, weaker, and searched the surface of the mitt in a frenzy until he found the evidence he'd always feared. There, along the cuff, he traced his son's initials.

THE END

MOHINI – GHOST OF THE TAMARIND TREE

by Shashi Kadapa

It was Amavasya, the night of the new moon. Darkness throttled the sky punctured by faint stars that glimmered through the clouds. A small group of villagers craned their necks, peering fearfully at the tamarind tree that loomed in the thicket. A figure in white swayed from a thick bough. They raised their kerosene lamps. The rope was taut around her broken and twisted neck, the eyes bulging and the tongue lolling. Faint anklets sounded in the night, the sweet smell of incense wafted in. Lyrics from a melodious Kannada folk song sounded haunting and soft.

They stood spellbound as the figure unraveled from the rope and swooped down at them. The sight was unnerving and they screamed and started running in terror. A youth from the group turned to look behind and saw the apparition floating and racing along as she whispered into his ears. He stopped, gripped by the spirit's spell. His friends shouted at him to turn his gaze and run. They found him early next morning rooted to the spot he had stopped, his eyes gouged out, his genitals ripped off, his face constricted in an intense orgasm. The dreaded ghoul Mohini had claimed another soul to quench her thirst for young men.

1. The legend of Mohini

The gathering at the Hanuman temple, the temple of the monkey face god, was frightened. The unexplained killing and rumors of Mohini were driving away business. Many of them were newcomers to the place and did not know about the legend. An old priest, Ramacharya, narrated the story one evening after the evening prayer at the temple.

"Many centuries ago, probably in the 8th century, when the great temples at Badami, Aihole, and Pattadakal were being built, there was an artisan, a master sculptor, called Krishnacharya. He supervised carvings of all the wonderful motifs, figures and gods in the temple. When the time came to carve the idol of the deity Banashankari, he was in a fix."

The gathering looked on with rapt attention.

Ramacharya continued "He wanted a virgin of perfect beauty. After searching far and wide he thought of his daughter Mohini. Accordingly, the statue of the deity was carved in her likeness. The king was very happy and bestowed riches and honor on Krishnacharya."

The people listened to him eagerly for they had never heard this tale.

Ramacharya sipped some water and continued "Soon after, the acharya moved to another village and lived peacefully. Everything went well until the time came for his daughter's marriage. A groom was found and the marriage ceremony was performed. Trouble started when the king came to know about the marriage."

One of the listeners interrupted "What was the trouble?"

Ramacharya continued. "The marriage ceremony was over and the couple were about to retire

141

to a consecrated room to spend their first night when the King arrived. He was very angry."

The king thundered "Oh, Acharya. How dare you marry off the girl? She is consecrated in the likeness of the idol of Devi Banashankari. She will have to remain unmarried and a virgin. She cannot have conjugal relations with anyone. I am ready to build a temple where she can stay and bless the devotees. My kingdom's riches will be placed at her feet. The Acharya refused to let his daughter waste her life. The king ordered his soldiers to enter the couple's room and drag them outside. The couple and Acharya were made to kneel before the king.

He shouted "This girl is a devi incarnate. None can touch or violate her. This is my order."

The old Acharya begged and prayed for mercy. He beseeched the soldiers and the youth of the village who he had helped many times to help. They were jealous of the old man and his wealth and laughed at the spectacle.

The king was merciless and firm. He dragged the groom aside and beheaded him. He ran his sword through the Acharya while Mohini was set free.

With his dying gasps the acharya placed a curse on the king. "My daughter will haunt this earth, seduce and kill young men. Your dynasty will end."

The girl ran away and hung herself on a tamarind tree.

Ramacharya continued "The Acharya's curse held true. The eldest son of the King died when a cobra bit him The second son, who was a toddler, disappeared, or was kidnapped and presumed killed. The king was slain in a battle, the city was conquered, and the dynasty soon ended."

"What happened to the girl?"

"No one knows for sure. Legends say that she turned into the evil spirit Mohini. She haunts orchards and wells, seduces young men and kills them. Sometimes, she enters the body of a woman, and makes her kill a young man. Over the centuries, this tale and the unexplained killings have continued."

The group returned to their homes, scared out of their wits. They locked their doors and decided to keep away from the thicket.

2. Fifty years on

Move forward 50 years, 1979. It was again the night of Amavasya and three children Shiva (Shivya), Kumar (Kumya), and Savita (Savti) studying in the 6th grade of KE Boards High School, Dharwad, stood at the periphery of a thicket of trees and shrubs. They had finished their tuitions late and wanted to reach home fast. The regular route was circuitous and meant walking an extra two kilometers. The short cut through the thicket reduced the distance to just a couple of hundred meters.

The thicket was a part of the Michigan family orchards, a fertile region with tamarind, coconut, guava, and other trees. The area was a part of Saptapur, a small suburb in Dharwad.

Kumar whispered, "Let's take the long route. I am scared of the forest and the large tamarind tree."

"Why?" questioned the impetuous Savita, a tomboy who loved to show that she was not scared of the dark.

Kumar answered, "I heard, that many years back, a woman hanging from the tamarind tree killed people. She is the evil spirit Mohini and she haunts the path under the tree. She and many other 'Duṣṭaśakti' evil spirits wait to catch anyone who passes under the tree and then kill them."

Savita said "I don't think any evil spirit resides in a tree on a dark night. It would enter a house and sleep on a warm bed."

Shiva stood silent unable to decide if the short cut was better than the long route.

Always a daredevil, Savita ran into the narrow footpath that went through the thicket. Shouting at her to come back, the other two followed reluctantly.

Crickets and other night insects chirped in the night, fire flies glowed as they flitted and sat on the bushes. As the children entered the thicket, there was a rustling sound and the branches moved to form a canopy overhead. The darkness and the trees

145

enveloped them like a blanket. The stars flickering overhead stayed hidden by the branches. The children moved abreast, holding hands for reassurance.

Suddenly, the crickets and the night insects went silent. There was a rustle of leaves and something in white hovered in the air in front of them. They could not make out the face; it was just a body covered in white, and it came close, looking at their faces.

Overcome with fear, the children opened their mouths to scream. Sheer terror turned their throats dry and they could barely utter a gurgle. Something cold and clammy touched their faces, their bodies, and then the specter disappeared rising into the darkness.

Their throats opened up and the children started screaming, standing rooted to the spot. The screams brought people out of their homes to help the children. It took a minute from when the figure swooped on the childrenfor the people to findthe children. They gathered the children in their arms and took them home. No one knew what had happened when the children were in the thicket. But all agreed that the children were in deep shock and incoherent when they were finally found.

*****

A young Vaidya, Guruji, practitioner of Ayurveda, attended to the children. It took a few days before the trembling children, all of them running a fever, could narrate their experiences. Savita was the worst affected and she would get up, scream, jump and attack people.

The children's parents met the Vaidya "Guruji, what happened to the children? What did they see in the thicket that scared them so much?"

"I spoke to them. It seems that they took a shortcut through the thicket and saw something in white that scared them."

The parents stood quietly absorbing the information. One of the women muttered, "It's Mohini. She has come to haunt the region."

The fever subsided after a few days; however, the incident remained dormant and deep in their

147

memories. After a few months, the children went away to different cities since their fathers took up new jobs or were transferred.

3. Death of the Vaidya

The young Vaidya was new to the region and had just started practice. He did not accept these urban myths and believed in science. Though he persistently asked people about this Mohini, they buttoned up and left him thirsting for information.

At last one of his patients gave him a clue. "Go to the public library, read the newspaper reports going back for more than 60 years. Also ask for the book on ancient ghosts."

*****

The public library on Subash Road was rambling and old with a musty odor. A few retired folks sat on the rickety chairs reading periodicals and newspapers. Guruji was known to the library staff.

"Namaskar. I want to read papers and books on Mohini."

The library staff went silent.

One of them queried. "Why does Guruji want to read about this Mohini?"

"Just interested."

They led him to some old dusty cupboards and pointed out some old newspapers. The oldest paper was the Mangalooru Samachara. It catered to proselytizing and spreading Christianity. The copies were old, faded, and not of much interest. There was one brief half column mention about an evil spirit called Mohini and she was blamed for unexplained deaths.

He read other newspapers and magazines and they intermittently spoke about deaths in the groves and orchards spread over hundreds of miles. He could make out that the authors were making fun of the myth and were speaking of the spirit very light-heartedly. There was mention of the legend of Mohini and the King, and decided that it was a fable, an urban myth.

He asked about the book and after much cajoling, the librarian handed the book to him.

He said. "Vaidyaji, this is the second time I am issuing this book. The last time was about 20 years back and the borrower died a horrible death. It has tantric incantations to summon ghosts and evil spirits. Please do not utter them aloud."

After finishing his duties for the day, the Vaidya sat in his room to read the book. He liked the place he lived in. The window looked over the vast Michigan orchards that belonged to the expatriate Michigan family who had decided to remain in Dharwad after independence.

The book was in Sanskrit. He could read and understand the language since he was an Ayurveda scholar. He went through the book and read descriptions of demons such as Yakshini, Muhnochwa, Nishi Dak, and Baak. After some searching, he found the section on Mohini.

The descriptions were very precise. "Be aware of Mohini, the evil incarnation of Devi Banashankari. She is evil, vengeful, and seeks tantric sex, tearing off the penis after consummation."

Engrossed, the Vaidya read further about how the demoness could be subdued through prayers to Vishnu. The text said that the spirit did not possess the great strength usually associated with evil spirits. She used her magical powers to seduce and kill. She would pick a region and haunt it for many years before moving on to another region.

He read further and saw one section on summoning the demon. A powerful urge gripped his soul and he started chanting the mantras to call the spirit. He ended with the invocation ॐ रोउम् रोउम् मोहिनचस्याय स्वाहा (Om Mohini| I welcome you).

The effort had drained out his energy and he flopped down at the desk. All of sudden, a Kannada song sounded in the background, the tune urging him to step out and walk. A strong fragrance wafted into the room. Blind to everything, he followed the song and the fragrance as it led him through the streets and into the thicket.

Mohini was waiting there under the tamarind tree, floating above the ground.

"O Vaidya. Why did you summon me?"

The tongue-tied vaidya, totally in her spell, moved forward. She opened her arms to grasp him to her breasts. His face dipped into her bosom and he realized that her dress was wet. She caressed his head and one hand reached out to his member. In the brief instant that he lost his life, he saw an eternity of the dead and the tortured in her soul.

The villagers saw him standing in the thicket, dead. His body and face were frozen in an intense orgasm, his member cut off.

*****

The district administration raised an inquiry into the death. Not wishing into entering controversies, they concluded that "the Vaidya had gone to collect herbs in the dark and died due to a snake bite."

Heeding the requests of the villagers, the government built a strong and high wall around the thicket and strung it with barbed wire. They posted signs warning people from entering the place. They wanted to chop down all the trees. However, none of the laborers were willing to risk the anger of the demoness by cutting the trees. The book was placed in a boc the strong room of the district collector and sealed and it would require the signed permit of a magistrate to access.

There were no killings after that and Dharwad grew to become a trade and manufacturing center. Everyone forgot about Mohini and the urban myth. People went by the longer path and some of them reported about a voice singing in the dark. Since the thicket was government property, no one entered or tried to encroach into the thicket.

4. The children grow up

Twenty years on, by 1999, the three children Shiva, Kumar and Savita were grown up. Shiva went to Pune where he completed his engineering studies and worked as a developer in an IT firm. Savita settled in Bangalore and had her own fashion design firm. Kumar remained in Dharwad and became a pujari. They had lost touch with each other in the 20 years since the incident at the thicket.

4.1 What Kumar was doing

Kumar performed pujas and other holy rituals from his base in Dharwad. He had taken a vow of celibacy and became a Brahmachari a person who has taken sacred vows of celibacy, wearing the dhoti, angavastram of a Brahmin, with his forehead and arms smeared in sandalwood paste. Alcohol, meat, and sex were taboo for him.

The local temple guardian priest conferred the honored title of Acharya on Kumar and he was now addressed as Kumaracharya. He was allowed to conduct all the brahmanical rituals of marriage, house warming, naming ceremony of new born, upanayana or the sacred thread ceremony, and death rituals where his prayers guided the soul of the dead to the other world.

One of the practices he indulged in was of talking to evil spirits. He also practiced अभिचरित exorcism a dangerous dark art. He had conducted a few sessions on exorcism and was gaining fame from his arts. This was a dangerous work and he knew that once an evil spirit was cast out of the victim's body, there was a chance that the exorcist would become possessed. However, his strict spiritual belief, rigorous penance and Brahmachari status protected him from such a possibility.

One incident got him worried. He had carried out an exorcism and had cast out the evil spirit of a malevolent widow from a young girl. When the spirit was brought out and branded with hot iron to ensure that it would not possess anymore, it had shrieked.

"Oh Acharya, You cast me out now and can laugh at my pain. But wait, a powerful spirit is waiting to vanquish you and she will hold you in eternity."

As was the usual practice, he studied his daily horoscope and the panchanga, the Hindu almanac. The configuration showed that Shani - Saturn was transiting the 12th house from the Moon, indicating that साढ़े साती seven and half years of misery, pain, death had started. He knew that it was beyond anyone's power to remove the obstacles. He had to face what came his way.

4.2 What Shiva was doing

Late for work, Shiva told his mother that he would have breakfast at the staff canteen. His mother came running with a plate of Idli and chutney urging him to eat. Shiva gobbled up a couple and ran out to catch the waiting company bus.

Shiva was now tall, handsome, glib, and enjoyed the attention of girls. He was the project lead, all his projects were successful, and his efforts were appreciated by the management. Only problem was that he was rather brash, bordering on arrogance and would plunge into a venture without thinking of the consequences.

In his sleep, he would often dream of a spirit standing in a forest, beckoning and crying out to him. There were also dreams of an ancient king, killing, and wars.

The spirit seemed to say "Come. It is time. I am waiting for you."

Memories of the dream would fade away after he woke up. When he mentioned these dreams to his mother, she would chide him.

"Stop watching the horror movies and TV serials. They are making you dream these wild dreams."

This was true since he was an avid horror media fan and would view all that he could get. However, many millions of people liked the horror genre. He was not sure if they also saw these images in their dreams.

His mother was worried. She remembered the incident at the thicket many years back and she knew the legend of Mohini.

She approached a नक्षत्रसूचक an astrologer, and narrated the story and events of the incident in the thicket. The Jyotish asked for Shiva's Kundali, the horoscope. He asked the lady to visit him again after two days.

The jyotishi astrologer began "As per my practice and the holy scriptures, I studied the time and date of his birth. There are many inauspicious celestial configurations in the kundali. At the time of his birth, the sun, the moon, and Rahu were in the first house in the sign of Virgo meaning that Rahu would eat the sun. Jupiter is in the 8th house of the moon. There is a very huge dosha, fault in his kundali."

Her brows knitted in an apprehensive frown, Shiva's mother asked "What Dosha?"

"The person is afflicted by Grahan Yog combined with Sarpa Dosh. Grahan or eclipse dosha means that unhappiness and misfortune will cloud over his future. Sarpa or snake dosha means that the wrath of the serpent god is active in his life."

"What will happen to my son?"

"These doshas appear when a person has committed grave sins in the past lives, killed women, Brahmins, and snakes. The person will be afflicted by deep memories of past sins, he will dream of such things, the memories will haunt him, and his sleep will never be peaceful. His soul is in search for a woman he wronged in the past. He will never marry in his quest for this soul."

"What will happen now?"

"It appears that some demoness or devi haunts his memories. Nothing can be done until she is satiated."

"What can I do?"

"I will make some amulets and give some mantras. Make him wear the amulets and recite the mantras when he takes an early morning bath and before he sleeps. He has to visit the Kukke Subramanya temple, the lord of all serpents, where the priests will remove the sarpa dosha."

Stiff with worry, she paid the jyotish and carried the amulets and mantras written on a piece of paper.

*****

She cajoled and threatened him to wear the amulets around his arm. She also made him take a picture of the mantra on his mobile and asked him to learn it by rote. She stood outside the bathroom when he took his bath and shouted at him to repeat the mantra. Same thing when he retired to sleep.

However, making him take leave and go to Kukke Subramanya in far off Karnataka state was going to be difficult.

Angrily he asked, "Amma, who told you this mumbo-jumbo about the amulets, mantras and visit to the temple?"

"I had gone to visit the Jyotishi. He studied your Kundali and he said that it was filled with ill omens."

"Really! How much did you pay him for his services?"

"One thousand rupees. He also knows the priests at the temple and will arrange for the stay and puja."

"Oh, great. How much does this package cost?"

"Well, he said 30,000 rupees. He will negotiate and bring it down."

"How kind of him! Amma, don't you see that this jyotish lives off gullible people like you. He read the Kundali and is able to see into my past life and the current one and predict what will happen! If he really has such powers he should become a stock broker and forecast stock prices. He will become very rich."

Outraged, she placed her finger on her lips and said "Sssh. You must not make such comments about gods and the demonic forces. I am very worried." Her mouth pouting, she said "I will fast until you agree."

Knowing how adamant his mother was, he knew that he had to agree. "I will ask in the office for four days leave. This can happen only after my project ends next month."

Smiling in contentment she agreed to wait.

*****

Shiva was not passionate about girls. He knew girls with whom he had lunch at the cafeteria and went out to movies, picnics, and dinner with other project friends. Many girls were attracted to him drawn by his good lucks, clean nature, and brilliance. However, he did not have any steady girlfriend though many girls wanted him.

Anita was one of the girls who fancied him. Try as she might, it never worked, and Shiva always circumvented the arrangement.

One day at the office she brandished movie tickets "See, I have two tickets for Star Wars: Episode I – The Phantom Menace."

On the first day, first show of release, tickets were impossible to get unless one was ready to pay a huge amount to scalpers, or if one knew the theater owners. Coyly she said, "You want to come?"

Attending the premiere would give Shiva huge bragging rights. Jumping at the opportunity he said yes.

Demurely and batting her eye lashes she asked, "Where do we meet?"

"At the theater entrance gate."

"There will be heavy crowds and we will miss each other. Can you pick me up from my hostel? I will be ready at 4 pm."

"That early? The show starts at 6."

"Yes. We can roam around on Fergusson College Road. I have some shopping to do. Then we can see the movie. You want to come or not?"

Hastily he agreed and reached her hostel by 4 pm. Anita had made sure that all the hostel girls were aware that she was going out with Shiva. The whole bevy of the hostel girls looked on jealously as she sat on his bike, wrapped her arms around his waist and they rode off.

They parked off Fergusson College Road and Anita spent time going over the wares. She wanted to be seen with him in public places, and all he did was constantly remind her that it was time for the show.

At last after much delay, they reached the theater, and Shiva was lost in the movie, the light-saber fights and the wonderful creatures. She tried to snuggle close to him but he sat uncaring and engrossed in the movie.

In the intermission, they went out bought some snacks and cold drinks. Anita excused herself to go to the bathroom. She locked herself in the toilet, finished, washed up, and flushed the toilet.

A fragrance filled the cubicle and a faint song started playing. To her horror, Anita found herself pulled to the toilet. She struggled, shouted and kicked the door until the attendant banged from outside and asked what was wrong. The force that held her was gone and she stumbled out disheveled, sweating, and panting.

She narrated her ordeal to the female attendant who assured her that the washroom was aired with room freshener, so fragrance was the norm. Yes, piped music was also played. About being pulled into the toilet, she pointed out the loose belt that Anita wore and remarked that probably the belt got snagged.

Rather subdued, Anita, disheveled and sweating, joined the impatient Shiva who was saying that the movie had started. She kept quiet through the movie. She was sure that something had wanted to drag her inside the toilet.

She was so morose and glum that she even turned down Shiva's offer for dinner.

*****

Anita tossed and turned, entering a fitful sleep. The glow of the date with Shiva had faded and now she felt empty and sorrowful. His body language and his total immersion in the film showed that he was not really interested in her.

She dreamt of a vision of a spirit that waved at her from a forest and she followed it. They stood under a huge tamarind tree and the spirit pointed up. A rope with a noose swayed softly. The spirit smiled and urged her with gestures to climb the tree and put the noose around her neck. It then made a motion of jumping. As Anita stood wavering, the face turned into a skeleton with the flesh peeling away and maggots wriggling out.

The spirit regained her beautiful form and said "Lay off. Stop. Shiva is mine."

Anita woke up trembling, drenched in sweat, and screaming with terror. Her roommate also woke, switched on the light to find Anita cowering in the corner, with the blankets pulled over her head.

The warden was called and she decided to take her to her quarters. She called up Anita's parents and they came, to take her home. The company was informed that she had gone on long leave due to ill health.

Shiva wondered what was going on. Anita was fine the previous evening. She went to the washroom and came out trembling. Now she had a nervous breakdown!

4.3 What Savita was doing

Savita was enjoying her success as a designer. She was slim, kept fit by gymming, trekking, and rock climbing. She was fair and had long tresses, something of a rarity in this day of the bobbed hair cut. She had a good voice and had trained as a classical Hindustani singer. Many boys tried to woo her, but all she did was talk nicely with them and kept them away.

Her specialty was ethnic wear and she created master designs for her collections. Her fans marveled at the ingenuity of the designs, the choice of fabrics, and the rich texture and weave of the fabrics. She had even received a few awards for her work. She admitted that she referred to books on history, studied scriptures, or rather got them translated into English, and that she drew inspiration from the carvings and motifs on ancient temples.

Right now she was busy assembling her collection for the spring season and was hunting for ideas. Reading some books, she found that a collection on ancient rural women would be a great idea. Accordingly, her designs ranged from simple wraps for the top and for the bottom, to the sari. Her showpiece was the Kaashtha or Nauvari, the 9-yard sari. Recurring dreams of a spirit that appeared in her dreams wearing the saree inspired the design.

She selected a soft, clingy, diaphanous white dyed silk, with elaborate flower borders, and a matching blouse. Though women in ancient India tied a cloth around their breasts, Savita considered a blouse to be more appropriate. She got the embroidery and other work done and decided to model it herself.

The collection was well-received and her showpiece got sufficient praise. When pressed about the inspiration for this apparel, she was in a fix and made up a story of seeing a spirit wearing this dress that appeared in her dreams. Well, all this was fodder for the press who lapped it up.

But disquiet ran through her mind. The dream was real, it would reoccur now and then. She had also started humming a Kannada song that she did not know. She did not mention this to anyone. Young and filled with success, she soon forgot and went around running her business and basking in the success.

5. The reunion

The management of KE Boards High School decided to celebrate an annual day of the school. As part of the event, all past students were sent invitations to attend the alumni gathering starting at 5 p.m. Kumar was one of the board members and they managed to track down old students and invited them. Many, including Shiva and Savita, accepted the invitations.

Shiva's mother was happy at this event. Kukke Subramanya temple town was just a few hours away from Dharwad and she would force Shiva to visit the temple. She decided to tag along. The great evening came, the gathering was well advertised and Savita and Shiva also attended.

Kumar was on the podium and made the valedictory welcome speech. Shiva and Savita sat some rows apart. She was wearing the showpiece 9-yard saree and was a stunner. They did not see each other until late in the evening due to the crowds.

Kumar's speech, or rather Kumar himself got their attention. Who was this fellow? Yes, this was Kumya, Kumar! What? He has become a pujari?

They then glanced around and, for a brief moment, they did not even recognize each other. Then suddenly smiles, waving, pointing fingers, and laughing silently. They waved and gestured that they would meet after the event.

The speech was followed by a long talk by the chairman and by other events. Then it ended with a thank you note and an invitation to have dinner.

Savita and Shiva could not speak clearly for the first few seconds. Words kept flying "What, where are you now? What are you doing? Where did you disappear?"

Kumar came to them as they sat on the chairs. "Namaskar. I hope you remember me?"

Kumar was wearing the dress of an acharya and carrying his bag with the holy books. They were deferent, standing up, and greeting him with a namaskar.

Waving his hands he asked them to forget it. "I am an acharya for the rest of the world. But for you two, I am still Kumya, so cut out the respect."

They laughed and joked walked around the small campus and the ground behind.

"You remember Kumya" said Shiva. "There was a hill here when we were studying. Our PT Teacher would make us dig the hill and we would wheel the debris in a wheel barrow and dump it on the side."

"Yes." broke in Savita. "I enjoyed sitting in the wheel barrow while you two pushed me to the land fill. It was fun."

They wandered, coming to a small well. Kumar said "Remember this well? Our watchman jumped into the well when the teachers found he had sold some sports equipment to fund his drinking and gambling debt."

She pointed out to an old building. "Remember that place? We went for tuitions there after school."

"Yes." said Shiva. "Then we went round that long route to reach home."

"Now I remember," broke in Savita. "Once we had gone through the thicket and fancied we saw a ghost. Let's retrace our path."

Against their will, Kumar and Shiva set out on the old trodden path. They stood at the beginning of the footpath, hesitant to venture into the space where they had experienced their worst fear.

Savita, still tomboyish, ran ahead and the other two shouted at her to come back.

6. The Final Encounter

The three went forward and came to the wall that the government had built long ago.

"Oh no!", cried Savita. "They have built a high wall. How far does it reach?"

"All the way around." remarked Kumar. "I was here when the wall was built."

"Oh. Okay. No way to get in, I suppose. Let's go back" remarked Shiva.

Kumar added "There is a way, a bit further down the left side. A well was in the way so a gap was left. The wall veers to the left, it is broken in some areas and we can climb in."

Cheerfully, Savita said "Great, let's go find that well and the gap."

The orchard owners had not sold the area and it remained filled with trees. Bats and owls flew overhead, hunting in the darkness. The night buzzed with crickets and other insects and they could see fireflies sitting on the creepers.

"This is enough." cried Shiva "Let's go back."

"No!" growled Savita. "We will push forward."

Kumar kept silent, holding his sack.

Savita seemed very determined to move forward as she gripped the branches and hoisted herself through small gaps in the underbrush that ran around the wall. The 9-yard saree allowed free movement. Besides, she was fit and moved fluidly.

They arrived at the well and the gap beckoned to them. The wall then turned sharply right and went beyond. They had to step carefully over the wall.

Savita went first, easily climbing the wall and jumping across. Kumar went next. The last was Shiva and his feet tottered as he looked into the waters, reflecting the moon. The dank smell of stale waters made him dizzy and he just barely managed to go across.

Kumar noticed that Savita's dress was wet, though she had not touched the water at any point. Her saree now clung to her thighs and breasts, outlining the perfect shape. In spite of his celibacy, he had to admit that she looked beautiful. Shaking his head, he chastised himself. He repeated his vows silently and brought his senses under control.

Shiva was having difficulty in adjusting to his surroundings. While he was a good IT programmer, a sedentary lifestyle and lack of exercise meant that he was not suited for even brief rough treks. He sat with Kumar on the grass to recover his breath.

"We are still outside the wall," remarked Shiva. "We still have to find a way over it."

"Yes. The wall has broken down some 20 meters inside. We can climb over."

"Why are you taking up this foolish journey? I have to go back to work when I return. If I break my leg, what will I do?"

*****

A couple of minutes had passed before they realized that Savita was not with them. Now where had she run off? The place was woody with thick grass and snakes were sure to be around. They shouted.

"Savita, Savti, where are you?"

"Here." answered a voice from the darkness. "Come on. Up this small footpath."

The footpath was just a small strip about eight inches wide, probably used by laborers who worked in the orchard. It ran around the wall and they went ahead. Savita stood at the broken part, climbed over and beckoned.

Shiva grumbled and muttered his anger. His idea of a thrill was to play a computer game. This clambering over a wall in a forest was too much.

Savita had again disappeared. She knew where to go even in this darkness. Shiva cursed himself for not bringing a torch. Now how was he to know that he would need one at a school alumni meet?

They clambered over the wall and stood, unable to decide where to go.

She called out again "Come on, just a few feet more. I am waiting."

They walked over the rough grass and saw her standing under the tamarind tree. Her dress glowed and shimmered in the moonlight. As they approached her a heavenly fragrance that reminded them of raat ki rani, night-blooming jasmine, wafted over them.

Savita started singing an old Kannada song, her sweet voice crooned over them, calming them with the soft melody. She stopped singing after the first few bars.

Unable to contain himself, Shiva bluntly said "Savti, it's too late. We have to go back. My mother is waiting at the hotel."

"Oh, let her wait, I have waited very, very long for this."

"What are you talking about Savti?" anger made his voice quaver. "You are speaking nonsense."

"Do you remember the incident at this place?"

Nonplussed, Shiva shook his head "What are you talking about?"

Kumar who had been silent all this time spoke up. "Yes. I know what you are talking about."

Ignoring Kumar, Savita brought up old memories. "Remember 20 years back when we three were taking a shortcut through this place. Do you remember a spirit in white swooped down on us?"

Long dormant memories returned to Shiva in a burst. Yes, he remembered, the ghostly apparition swinging down this tree. She had floated before them. He remembered the cold and clammy fingers touching his face, feeling his chest, then his genitals. Then the spirit had moved over Kumar and then it had stood in front of Savita gazing deep into her eyes, it appeared to kiss her and then it swopped back and disappeared. He remembered everything now.

He gasped and stuttered. "Yes, I remember. What did it do to you, Savti?"

Kumar spoke out "It first examined our face to see if we had a beard or moustache, and then it touched our genitals to see if we were men she could seduce. Finding us still children she left and approached Savita, studied her and entered her body. What you see now is the spirit of Mohini in Savti's body. She enters her body and leaves when she wants."

"What?" cried Shiva.

"Yes, Shiva. This," he indicated Savita,"is Mohini in her incarnation. She will seduce and kill you, then Savita and then go in search for another male. Her thirst is insatiable."

"How true Acharya" Mohini spoke sweetly through Savita's body, the voice dripping and husky with erotic intent.

"Oh no, Mohini. You cannot touch me. I am a bramhachari, protected by the power of Lord Brahma, the creator of the world."

"Yes, I know. I do not want to sully myself with your brahmachari blood, though I have had many in my centuries of pleasure with people from your creed. I will use Shiva for I have waited many eons for this."

Kumar sat on the ground, pulled out a small copper cup, the Panch-Patra, and an Araghi, spoon that he used for religious ceremonies. Then he broke open a sealed container that had ganga jal, water from River Ganga, and poured some of it into the cup.

"Shiva!" shouted Kumar. "This thing will call you. Try to resist with all you have. Block out your eyes and ears to her. Stand still and do not move. I will call the gods and we will hold her captive in the spell. Then we can imprison her forever."

Kumar began his mantras, praying for protection against the evil spirit.

ॐ त्र्यम्बकं यजामहे

सुगन्धिं पुष्ठिवर्धनं

उर्वारुकमिव बन्धनान्

मृत्योर्मुक्षीय मामृतात

(Oh Lord Traiambaka, our savior, please protect me from the evil spirit)

Savita Mohini laughed at him and said "You forget that I am the daughter of an acharya. I have chanted mantras for protection against charlatans like you."

She turned towards the cowering Shiva who sat huddled on the forest floor, covering his eyes and ears.

"That is of no use. I do not need your eyes or ears, only your mind."

"Kumar!" screamed Shiva. "Why is this thing after me?"

"She probably thinks you are the long lost heir of the King who killed her father and husband."

Slowly she started gaining control of Shiva's mind, cell by cell rocked with sensuous pleasure so infinite that he wanted to give up to them. He was opening up to the fragrance and the song that she was humming.

Shiva had spent years studying hard in the hostel even when his roommates played loud music. He could focus and concentrate on his work even when surrounded by chattering coworkers and beautiful girls.

He remembered Anita in the theater, strained and troubled from the episode in the washroom. He fought back, focusing on her face and her voice. Then he remembered his mother and the mantras he was forced to recite.

Shiva began shouting the mantras out. The spirit felt her power weakening and turned up all her strength to conquer his mind.

Kumar had started invoking the strongest devis and devas.

ॐ विश्वाय नाम गन्धर्वलोच्नि नामि

लोउसतिकर्नै तस्मै विश्वाय स्वाहा

औं महा-धेट्यै

च विद्महे दुर्गायै

च ढिमहें

थान्नो धेवी प्रचोदयतः

ॐ ह्रीं बगलामुखी

सर्व्दुष्तनं वाचं मुखं पदं

(Om, I invoke the Devi Mata Durga who is daughter of Kathyayana, Oh, devi, give me higher intellect and enlighten me.

Oh Lord, grant me the power to destroy the minds of a thousand evil spirits.

Oh Three-eyed Lord Shiva who has the supreme bliss and sustains all living things. Please help me to liberate this soul)

"Shiva!" Shouted Kumar. "She is weakening and she will soon leave Savita's body. For a brief instant she will be exposed in her physical and vulnerable state. I will catch her then. You pick up Savita and lead her out."

Mohini was physically weak. She could only gain control over the mind of vulnerable and mentally unprepared men. When her sensuous and erotic powers were impeded, she could do nothing. For the first time in many centuries, she was defeated and her anger was untamable.

Screaming ancient curses, she withdrew from Savita's body. Then she turned towards Kumar who was still uttering the mantras. Without a break, Kumar grabbed the Ganga water pot and rushed towards the wraith that stood shimmering, partly in her spirit form and partly in her human form. Her spirit form was beautiful while her physical form was a dried and withered skeleton and the jaws stretched open to curse.

Grabbing her, he threw the holy water down her bony jaws. The spirit violently struggled and screamed, then started fading. Her last act was to bow to Kumar in a deep namaskar, thanking him for liberating her soul.

The trio trudged back the way they had come and went to the alumni gathering. Savita was weak and could hardly walk. The gathering was almost over. Hurriedly they got into Shiva's car and drove off to the hotel.

*****

Shiva's mother was not satisfied with the lame explanation that Savita was not feeling well. She made her sleep on her bed and started asking questions to Shiva and Kumar.

"Who is this girl? Why was she so disheveled? Did they do anything to her? Where are her parents? Is she married?"

Shiva sat back on the sofa totally spent and let Kumar give all the explanations.

Amma finally asked "How did you know what mantra to chant and to make her drink Ganga Water?"

"Well, Amma" said Kumar. "After our encounter 20 year back, my mother's brother, the Vaidya, was killed by Mohini. I grew up and learnt the scriptures. My uncle appeared in a dream and explained what had to be done. Essentially, she was an insatiated spirit. Her funeral rites were not performed, and she was not given Ganga water when she died.

As per our Hindu rituals, a few drops of Ganga water is given to the dying so that they attain moksha, salvation. If this is not done, then the atma the soul of the departed will be suspended in the patalloka, the nether world.

I included some funeral mantras in our fight and forced Ganga water down her throat. Her spirit is now free and she thanked me for liberating her.

"Is she gone forever?"

"Well Amma, I think so. However, one cannot be sure of ancient spirits. At least our Savita is free."

"Kumar" broke in Shiva's mother "What did you get out of this? You risked your life and would have suffered in the nether world if she had overpowered you."

"Amma, I am a Brahman. Mohini's salvation freed hundreds of souls from the nether world, including my Uncle's, that she had consumed over the centuries. Besides, it is the duty of a Brahman to care for the spiritual needs of people. I only did what is expected of me."

"What next?" asked Shiva.

"Up to you two. If you two decide to get married, I would like to have the honor of performing the marriage."

THE END

AND THE DARK

Some things are best forgotten.

Other things never should be.

DONE, AND DONE AGAIN...

by Sergio 'ente per ente' Palumbo

with edits by Michele Dutcher

"Alone, alone, all, all alone,

Alone on a wide wide sea!

And never a saint took pity on

My soul in agony…"

from *"The Rhyme of the Ancient Mariner"*

-Samuel Taylor Coleridge

The first time it happened had been during a storm that hit the coastline near the port of Sarandë, Albania, which was his native country. Laert Dushku remembered that very well.

It was about nine A.M. and the ship was approaching the point of the high sea from which the route would change, according to his maps, to head towards his destination which would take him one day, more or less, weather permitting. The 500 TEU Feeder-Max container vessel named Vjollca that he captained serviced some medium ports of the Eastern Mediterranean Sea, especially in Greece, Albania, and Turkey. He journeyed forward without any real difficulties and the sun could be seen in the sky, though it looked pale because of some sparse clouds that were visible in the distance.

Laert knew that his sea-craft, with its 12 crewmen, was not one of the largest vessels that crossed that stretch of water, as there were only a few merchant ships smaller than this one these days. Other than that, the Vjollca was older than most and the 40-year-old man was also aware that a new generation of feeder vessels was ready to take that route over, for sure. But for now, this was his job and his route and he was content with that.

It had taken him a long time to become captain, with years of sacrifice, exhausting duties on smaller vessels of dubious renown and reliability, wakeful nights and great care, of course. Anyway, he finally had been commissioned to that ship and had been appointed as captain when he was 38.

Vessels like that were specifically designed for their trade purposes: their open-top hold design insuring swift loading operations. Their ship also provided electricity for up to 40 reefer containers. In order to sail year-round without problems, they were built to very high standards, at least at the beginning. But the fact was that this one had become a bit outdated nowadays, having reached the considerable age of 40, and there were some problems with parts of the hull and the prow. But overall it was still in pretty good shape, all things considered, and was perfectly capable of achieving what was required of it. With its great stowage flexibility and a high-speed service, the Vjollca was suitable for transporting large quantities of 24.5 by 49 foot containers. Its powerful 4,825 KW engine easily moved its 265 foot length and its full load with no trouble and was absolutely seaworthy, always passing inspections and the periodical tests that were routine from time to time.

However, what they had to undergo that day, just in a matter of a few hours from that moment, could never have been expected…

Laert Dushku had gotten used to always standing, usually wearing his off-white uniform while he was aboard. Anyone could tell from first sight that he was a sailor, or someone who worked on a ship and that he was also accustomed to traveling across the sea. Maybe it was his spiky fair hair that was always a sort of mess and his narrow blue eyes - the same color of the ocean on a sunny day – which made him look the part. Or perhaps it might be due to the hardened expression he always wore, the look of somebody who had been navigating for most of his life. He had always been famous among his friends and several acquaintances of his for his typical smile, since he was a lanky kid with long hair, but his smile had become rarer and rarer since those strange events had taken place.

The unusual shaking had started inside of him rather than on his skin, that first day, which was completely unexpected. Also the first signs of the incoming storm that had been spotted in the distance hadn't been predicted either and, if you had asked him for his opinion, he would have sworn that today was supposed to have been a day with fair weather, at least according to his past experiences.

He had noticed the storm approaching from the tall wheelhouse of the vessel which held the navigation and communications equipment of the ship, having been left alone for a moment as his second-in-command had just gone out to enjoy a smoke. Then, things went from bad to worse.

The hairs started standing up on the back of his neck, his heart beat four times faster than normal, and his stomach felt like he'd swallowed fire. Shortly thereafter, he was unable to control himself, as if he was under the rule of something else, something very different from his own mind. His throat started giving out some guttural noises, and he spoke in a language he had never heard before. This wasn't his voice!

In fact, there was only a very small part of his mind that was still aware of what was happening around him. Laert immediately believed that he had become a completely different person. He didn't have a name for that new being then, although he has one now.

The cold wind increased, becoming very strong, all the elements seemed to have taken a turn for the worse and the situation deteriorated very quickly. If he had been outside, in the open, he would have unwillingly danced along like a girl at the fair. The saltiness coming into the wheelhouse from the taller and taller waves was unrestrainedly beating against the sides of the ship and encrusted everything on the decks, including the load of containers. The unusual scarcity of light caused by the low dark clouds had almost made it difficult to look at the sea ahead. How could such rough water have erupted out of nothing?

When the dangerous outcrop was spotted nearby, it was already too late and a collision course was clear. Was this what the captain really wanted? It was hard to say given his very low oversight, and his lack of control over himself.

There was not enough time to attempt to steer his way clear of the outcropping. Even if some of the crew had suddenly rushed into the wheelhouse, pushing him aside to reach the control panel, They probably would have been unsuccessful at veering away, trying to reach the safety of the open sea. The captain was simply incapable of saving the ship at that moment, and time was running out quickly.

His hands and his actions were making the vessel head for the coastline at full speed, through that storm, but it was not his mind, not his free will. This out-of-body experience wasn't something he would remember for long, anyway, and he would later have no suspicions about his behavior that day. How could he?

As his fingers were clinging onto the helm with a sort of unbelievable superhuman strength - insomuch that if he had been restrained with shackles, he could have quickly made them fall into pieces - the man could barely hear himself breathing, and he wasn't certain that his heart was still beating.

The symptoms he presently showed off seemed to have come on without warning: seized by a violent behavior, his body was wracked with painful convulsions, and the unearthly screaming that came out of his mouth escaped human understanding.

There was the clangor of the metallic bulwark as it ran, full-speed, against the underwater rocks, the cries of the other crewmen outside, the jerking of the deck under the crewmen's feet, and things thrown here and there on the tables and on the shelves before falling down and hitting other objects. These were recollections that were deeply engraved in his memory as the hull below burst open, seawater coming in at a distressing speed through its many tears. These memories made him feel the terror all over again whenever he thought about the blood-curdling moments on the Vjollca before everything became completely dark to him.

After that disaster - that had caused the deaths of six men in his crew - they had found him in desperate condition, though alive, in what was left of the wreckage. He had stayed with the ship, as every good captain should do, but not because he had a choice in the matter. He simply couldn't do anything else, nor could he, at that moment, take any useful actions. It had been one of his crewmembers, Avni, who had come to save him, as he himself was out of his mind, tired, and disoriented, as he would be told later. His recollections were extremely distorted, he was incapable of reasoning or moving, his mouth spoke strange words that he, Avni, and the others couldn't comprehend. He couldn't be understood, not even when he had been brought aboard a lifeboat nor in the hospital.

For weeks, his conditions did not improve and the local physicians didn't know what else they could try on him. Possibly, this was a case of strange mental health disorder that had appeared suddenly, though they had never witnessed something like this before. Avni had stayed by his bedside for several days following the crash.

Then, one of his former crew had thought of something they could try and Avni had agreed. A priest was called and had come to his bed. They suspected his problems were demonic in nature, or the activity of the devil…

"Exorcizamus te, omnis immunde spiritus, omni satanica potestas, omnis incursio infernalis adversarii, omnis legio, omnis congregatio…"

Those words were spoken, under the faint light of a lamp, and the voice of the priest still ruled over his mind and remained in his ears. Laert remembered every syllable he had heard.

Finally, things had returned to normal, in a way, after the priest had completed what was required of him.

He was later told that he had undergone an exorcism, as a priest had practiced it on his body so as to have it freed. Once it was certain he fully comprehended what he had heard, he remembered he said, "Really? Was I exorcised? Why…?" He reported that he had no memory of the symptoms he had experienced while in the wheelhouse of the vessel.

"We don't know why it came to that, but this was what we thought you needed at that time. And this is what that priest did when we called him to you. It worked! You should be happy about that!" Avni had uttered this in his typical low tone, ruined by too many years of smoking.

"I'd better talk to that priest. Do you know where he lives?" Laert had asked his friend.

And so, four days later, he had went there.

*****

The weather was clear that morning, while the man was driving and thinking about everything that had previously occurred. He had been hospitalized, then exorcized, and then there had been a set period of convalescence before he could go back to the offices of the sea company he worked for, if he felt alright. What Laert still found strange, or actually unexplainable, was that the sea had immediately started to fall calm when the disaster was over. This was according to the reports the locals living on the coastline had made about the incredibly bad storm that he had survived that terrible day. The captain himself had heard some of them say so. He knew a few of them in person and he didn't doubt their recounts. Which turned everything into an even more unusual occurrence.

And this left him still unprepared for what he was about to find out when he got to the house of that priest.

After Laert parked his car, he checked his watch while walking up the path that brought visitors, and usually believers, to the house of Father Prek. His tiny rectory was situated next to the small church that was still being used for the religious activities. When the seaman was told he was not there, he tried to find him in the old church nearby. And there he found him. The father stood next to the Bishop's throne which was made of marble, not far from the white walls of the church that surrounded it on all sides.

Laert had no need to introduce himself as Father Prek recognized his face as soon as he appeared before him.

"I know you...I freed you from what was afflicting you, while you were hospitalized," the almost bald bearded religious man told Laert.

"What did you do to me there? Can you tell me what happened, please?"

"You were exorcised, it's as simple as that…" Prek replied. "I drove an evil demon out of you that was inhabiting your body."

"How is that possible, father?" the captain asked. "Why did it happen to me? I mean, I'm a believer, maybe not a practicing one, but I have never considered possible the existence of demons, or creatures like them…"

"The signs were self-evident and I had no doubt about your possession when I saw you. Your friends acted well to call me for help. Unfortunately, demons can sometimes enter humans to use their bodies as if they were their own."

"Couldn't it have merely been that I was under a great deal of stress, or perhaps I was showing early signs of mental illness? Maybe I experienced a momentary loss of reasoning, possibly I had hit my head and that might have intensified my stress in some way unbeknownst to me? That wouldn't have been demonic influence… sorry if I speak this way, but I just can't wrap my head around what happened and I'm afraid of the things I don't understand…things like these. I am trying to figure out all of this, you see." Laert had openly explained his thoughts, because he wanted to be able to calm down, to be protected from his deepest worries.

"The evil demon that was in your body was driven out of you thanks to my intervention. That is exactly what happened."

"But how is that even possible? How could such a wicked creature have been in my body, in the first place? I did nothing wrong!" The captain's voice was uncertain now and a little sad.

"This kind of shipwreck already happened here in the past, in this stretch of the sea…at least, according to what my predecessor told me once," that priest revealed.

"What? When…?"

"There are recounts of old exorcisms by the man who ran the church here, before I arrived and replaced him when he retired because of his decrepitude. He wrote about the events in his diaries because he thought they might turn out to be useful someday," the other man added in a low voice. "About sixty years ago, a large steamship wrecked in these same waters, and it was a huge disaster. The crews at that time were far larger than they are nowadays, with all the modern instrumentation that you modern sailors have, and there were also many who were lost at sea during the storm. A demon was said to be involved in that, it wasn't only the incredibly bad weather that caused it. Or maybe the deadly storm itself was caused by that unholy creature."

"Why should that tragedy be connected to the shipwreck of my vessel?" Laert asked him.

"The diaries indicate a horrific storm had suddenly arisen on what had been a calm day, and it had disappeared soon after, in an unexplainable way, as strangely as it had come. And a maritime disaster occurred..." Prek continued.

"Shipwrecks may happen at sea. It was more common in the past when there were steamships or wooden sailing ships, but it still occurs today, even with modern vessels. Storms also happen, I've seen a lot of them during my travels..."

"The circumstances reported in the recounting of those other shipwrecks look suspiciously similar to what happened to you and your crew." the priest looked at him closely. "And then there is the way you behaved: your words full of nonsense, and your voice –lacking in warmth and biting - that was not really yours at that time. As a matter of fact, I'm sorry to tell you that there is no way to have such a possession recognized as a psychiatric or medical diagnosis. Physicians regard these occurrences as mental diseases, at all times. But for me the answer to this mystery can only be found in religion and beliefs. And I usually regard such possessions as a genuine condition, if I spot the proper symptoms…"

It took Laert some moments before the seaman accepted what he was being told. He knew that this was exactly what his second-in-command Avni, and the others, had revealed to him about his conditions when he was discovered in the wreckage. He also knew that his strange behavior had lasted even later, when he still was hospitalized. "What is this demon? Why did it take over my body in the first place?"

Alrinach is the demon's name, Father Prek told the captain, and it was somehow connected, in an unknown way, to the shipwrecks. The creature seemed to be ageless and every time it appeared, disasters and death at sea occurred. "Also the ancient pagans spoke of such a presence, calling it Aldinach as well. It was the devil under many different shapes, I'd say…" the priest explained.

Now Laert knew the name of it. However, too many questions still remained incomprehensible to his mind. Why had it taken over his body? Why did such an unearthly evil thing, come out of the waves, like one of those terrible creatures from the deep that were talked about in legends? It had been reported that in the old times such creatures changed color to blend in with the darkness and then suddenly appeared to drag people in the night... Did it live in the so-called midnight zone, where no sunlight reached below 3,300 feet, a hidden underwater area, a place where the sea was dark and freezing cold? Why did it enter his human body, towering out of the liquid surface at once, like a hunter ready to seize its prey as if dinner was being served?

"Why me?" a dejected Laert asked the religious man.

"Unfortunately, this is something I can't tell you. I don't know how, or why. Though, at times, such things occur with no fault of the poor target of the demons. Such invasions by disembodied evil beings may take place even if you are not a sinner, actually," a saddened priest nodded with a regretful face.

*****

Located in the southern part of the Albanian Riviera, the coastal city of Sarandë was not very large. It had always been small throughout its history, at least as far as Laert knew, and it probably wasn't going to change. Its name came from an ancient Byzantine monastery, its shape owing much to the old Venetian influence in the region. There was still a large Greek population in the town, regardless of the apparently unceasing emigration to Greece. The experienced eye was able to recognize at once the countless bays, beaches, and mountains that surrounded the urban area.

Near to Sarandë stood the archaeological remains of the ancient city of Butrint. What could be said about the city itself? There were one or two highly recommended lavish restaurants that served seafood but the seaman had never been inside, though he had spotted them many times while walking down the boulevard in the heart of the city. There were a lot of bars open year-round for drinks right on the beaches. Of course, he had often frequented those! Beyond that, there were many grills cooking great sqepasti and some traditional Albanian main courses that he enjoyed, small venues that had benefitted recently from an increase in tourists. Family tourism and seasonal work during the summer period helped mitigate the local unemployment rate. Cruise lines were not allowed to dock at the port. Instead, a speedboat ferried tourists back and forth between cruise ships and the port itself.

What else could be said about the town? Not much, except it was his home. This was the place that Laert had always come back to over the course of his life whenever he was not aboard a vessel, or busy elsewhere while waiting for his next ship to embark. The seaman loved that part of the country, with its over 300 sunny days a year and a typical Mediterranean climate. On the other hand, he wasn't in love with the rare, dark, and powerful storms that happened at times, particularly in November and December. He feared them now more than ever, deep in his grieved heart. And not only for the dangers involved in navigation, or for the very disastrous consequences that could occur along the coastline. He feared the storms for what they brought along with them, and what they could mean for his personal life. They never brought anything beneficial, nothing pleasing, just suffering and sorrow. He knew those troubled feelings very well by now.

It had been a year since the bloody wreck of his Vjollca. Perhaps it would be better to say, since the wreck of his ship because of his insane actions. and all that he had undergone during those terrifying minutes of his life when he had unexplainably been out of his mind. He was walking the street to the port where his destination stood. After all he had gone through and having been removed from the list of captains of the sea company he previously worked for, it had only been thanks to a friend of his that he had been hired for another job.

The venues were alive with lights, local music, and the laughter of those that stood inside. The seaport seemed to be expanding, thanks to the tourists, in other areas of entertainment to attract visitors and some small companies had started offering the newcomers interesting services to entice them to visit the area and the coastline from the sea. One of those had bought an old luxury yacht that was two decades old, the date of launch being 2001. It had once been used by a businessman from Northern Europe, who had now reconditioned it for new purposes. Powered by diesel engines, this ship was called Yllka and had a length of 190 feet with a crew of just six men. Its legal occupancy was 40 passengers, ready with their cameras and camcorders to film whales or other interesting sea-life, if they spotted them in that stretch of sea. The yacht had a large observation deck, free Wi-fi and a luxury inside area with a bar. To Laert himself, this vessel seemed a little old but it had been properly maintained and was in acceptable working condition.

Of course, his pay had greatly diminished now that he wasn't a captain of a large Feeder-Max container vessel anymore, serving only as second-in-command on his new boat, but at least it was a job, something to pay his monthly bills. And he hadn't been forced to be grounded forever, which would have been very dejecting for a sailor like him. The man had tried several times to find a better job, but he knew that when people in charge of a company discovered that he had been involved in such a wreck, with everything that had happened and all those fatalities, they simply, and reasonably, kept him at a distance. He had heard such justifications too many times, so he didn't bother trying too hard anymore. Damn them, he thought. What kind of fool did they take him for? He sighed in frustration, well aware that he had still to consider himself lucky that he was, at least, still aboard this yacht for tourists.

Every time he was on that yacht he felt free, as if he was busy doing something important where he could put his experience at sea to good use. On the other hand, every time he sailed he always brought his deepest worries with him. And his fears about what might happen, one day or another. Again…

They never had any major problems while they were at sea, if you overlooked the tourists who got seasick at times, or their children, and the great amount of trash they usually left on the viewing deck. After all, if the crew had been on a smaller and less comfortable boat, things would have proven much worse for them. These small grievances were nothing compared with the command crew's duties on the Vjollca: the constant necessity to be on guard due to his old ship's load made up of containers, and the long naval routes it sailed across the Mediterranean.

The 60-year-old graying captain of the Yllka, named Kuzman, looked professional to the seaman, though a bit aged, and maybe a little heavy. Perhaps this captain had not had many other chances at getting a better job recently as well. These local trips were also assisted by tour-guides, who could help the passengers find animals and interpret their behavior while they looked for and tried their best to identifying the different types of whales they spotted. Tourists were also handed a Whale Identification Sheet during orientation which helped them spot the more common marine animals along the route.

There was a complimentary open bar for soft drinks and beer, and food was usually served as well. Whales weren't always seen during the short three-hour trips and the crewmen were used to that situation, but at times it happened and the animals surrounded the Yllka, nosing about and playing in front of the bow for an unforgettable experience.

Laert watched as the tourists were helped aboard and asked to take a seat. Then they retracted all moorings, and the order "Dead slow ahead!" was heard as the boat distanced itself from the pier and they headed towards the open sea.

'You'll grow out of it…' the seaman thought, as he tried to push his sad memories to the back of his mind. "Laert, take the helm for half an hour…" the older captain told him at a certain point during the navigation, in an unexpected turn of events. "I spotted an acquaintance of mine among the tourists aboard and I want to chat with her…"

For a moment, a deep worry overcame the man, and he didn't reply immediately. Then, he heard the voice of Kuzman again. "What is going on, Laert? Are you okay?"

At that moment they were at about the halfway point in their sea tour and the coastline was well visible behind the rear of the yacht. He knew he had to say something but he was also afraid of what might happen.

"Aye, aye, sir…" he exclaimed, in the end. And so he approached the helm, doing as ordered by the captain.

Things went well, anyway, despite Laert's growing fears as the boat moved forward under his guidance. For a while.

As they approached their third short stop at sea on their trip away from the coastline, set to let the tourists take their best pictures, the weather conditions plainly changed. The significant disruptions to the previous weather conditions appeared immediately clear, at least to a sailor like him, such as stronger and stronger winds. Then some large threatening storm clouds came into view, that quickly surrounded their area and an awful downpour fell upon them all in a matter of minutes.

It had all happened so quickly that there was no time to give the "Batten down the hatches" order with the aim of preparing for the worst weather, by securing the closed hatch covers with wooden battens so as to prevent water from entering from different angles. The freeboard above the waterline started changing at an unbelievable rate. That storm that had blown up unexpectedly, against any weather forecast, and it promised to become worse by the minute.

The yacht became a fast-moving vessel that now jumped over the water instead of pushing through it. And the expected righting couple - that was the force which tended to restore a ship to equilibrium once a heel had altered the relationship between her center of buoyancy and her center of gravity – was of no help.

If Laert had been afraid of the consequences of a staggering and unexpected storm while he was aboard the massive Vjollca, he was now in full bedazzlement given the small size of the present yacht they were on. The helm was under his command during these moments only by chance, which was the same thing that had happened that day so long ago, when the wreck of his large ship had taken place not far from the shoreline.

He felt an attack of irrationally obsessive thoughts. He couldn't tell if this was because of his fears, or if these thoughts came from somewhere else, something that was entering his soul again. He began acting in a strange manner.

The captain was running back to the Command deck and talking to Laert, openly dressing him down because he would not reply, but he almost couldn't hear what the captain was crying out as he looked lost now, or prey to something unknown. More than that, the man was completely unable to command his own body and do as he was ordered… Kuzman looked uncertain as he noticed his incomprehensible behavior.

Some disconnected and contradictory orders were heard in the meantime, like "Hard-a-port!", "Midships!" or also "No more maneuvering!". But it was already too late… Laert at the helm, was following some strange thoughts he had, and his mind and gestures were no longer his own.

The portion of the yacht's hull that was partly submerged and partly brought above water by the rolling of the vessel, called 'Between wind and water', behaved as if it was in turmoil due to the increase in sea level and the vessel itself, at times, listed at 40 degrees or more. This could only result in the sinking of the boat itself soon, which meant it would probably reach the bed of the sea today.

What the man found strange, when he finally was aware of it, was that he was foaming at the mouth. He also could hear his heart beating four times faster than usual. He was completely unable to control himself, as if he was under the rule of something else again, and he began to speak in guttural noises. A desperate Laert could almost feel the changes in his vocal intonation and facial structure. Seizures and trembling very soon overcame him and he started thinking of himself as if he was overwhelmingly strong and uncontrollable while he was aboard the Yllka.

He recognized that voice, which obviously wasn't his…Laert suddenly realized that he had become a completely different person, again.

He noticed that he was keeping the helm in his hands, and also saw clearly the course he was following, against the rules of navigation, clearly indicating that he was heading for the coastline. At that speed, it seemed that he wanted to run aground! It was as if sinking the boat full of people because of the storm wasn't enough for him - another deadly wreck was what happened to be in his mind now and was what he actually desired!

The collision course alarm began blaring across the decks, but there wasn't much that could be done, given the mind-boggling storm they were in and their horrifying situation. There wasn't any way to remove the huge amount of water that kept entering the boat because of the powerful breakers that looked like ocean waves more than the typical storm swells of the much smaller Mediterranean Sea.

Life-vests began to be handed out to the tourists, but the captain doubted that they would have enough time to put them on. The desperate faces of the passengers clearly showed that a planned evacuation of the vessel was out of the question, provided that getting into that tormented water below was extremely dark because of the ominously overcast sky. The crew was afraid that there was no way to get all of them to safety in case the ship needed to be abandoned at once, and that nothing could keep those tourists afloat even for a short time.

The most troublesome thing was that keeping them safe aboard that hopping yacht under those prohibitive conditions was impossible, and, on top of this, Laert was forcing the ship to follow a deadly course that would kill them all soon. How could he do this again? From what deep dark place inside his head did the unbelievable strength he had now come from?

They were approaching the shoreline so quickly that there was nothing anyone could do to stop the disaster from happening.

When they abruptly hit the first protuberance of the low cliff, some of the crew died immediately, the captain sustained head injuries and many passengers were plunged into the sea, never to be seen alive again.

Again, on this occasion, another crewman who was left alive by chance found Laert all in one piece after the bloody wreckage, as soon as the very unusual storm had subsided. There was a terrible pain low on his right side. He found it hard to get his breath.

Many long weeks after he was hospitalized again, with no explanation about his strange condition, something happened.

And Father Prek came to him again, in order to do his duty once more.

*****

After Laert left the hospital, while still having some minor pain in part of his body, he spent several months alone.

He had been told that such a thing could occur again, and that having been freed once didn't mean that he would be free from the demon forever. For some unknown reason that damn' creature had chosen his body as its receptacle, and there was no certainty that the sailor could live without any worries in the future. It had already happened twice before… Other than that, now everyone in the area knew that he had been at the helm of two sea-craft that had been destroyed while they were near the coastline of his home port.

He had been told that the old recounts revealed that such ancient creature might come back into the body of the unfortunate person it had chosen, and that the demon's possessions might happen several times, using its victim for its own evil purposes. This made things more complicated, and also deepened his fears, undoubtedly.

He had survived, but what was really left of him, of the man Laert once was, before all of this had happened? When was it going to take place again? Was it good if he wanted to go and sail at sea another time, even by himself?

And, most of all, he wondered what it would be like if next time he never regained consciousness long enough to return to being himself. What if on the next occasion he changed forever, being turned into a madman whose actions weren't his anymore?

In the following months, he stayed at home most of the time, where only silence and darkness greeted him. He had also become accustomed to getting into a wooden cabinet, taking a glass and a bottle of Skënderbeu, and pouring himself a generous measure of alcohol. However, even that didn't remove the growing anger he felt in his mind, being only a breath away from tears. Now he had the time to rest for a while and think of the heart of the whole damn problem itself.

Until the next time happened, of course… for it always found its way back to him.

THE END

DEAD MAN'S HAND

by C.R. Langille

I took a seat in the corner of the Billy Brock's Saloon making damn sure my back was toward the wall. I had already been shot once today and I wasn't looking to get bushwhacked while I was bending an elbow or playing cards.

The saloon was a small hole-in-the-wall building with an actual hole in the wall. Dust covered everything no matter how much Billy tried to keep the place in order. I reckon it was due to the endless sea of dirt and sage just outside the walls.

I didn't much like the place, but it was familiar, and familiar was what I needed. I'd played cards many times in Billy's establishment, hustling anyone willing to gamble with me. I was good at poker, but I was better at ensuring I'd win. Sometimes you had to lose a bit, get the other players comfortable, and then spring the trap.

The sun blasted everything outside in an unbearable heat, which made everything inside stuffy. I wanted to take my coat off but wasn't about to advertise the fact that I had been shot.

"Hey there, Jack, what'll it be?" Billy asked.

"The usual."

There weren't many folks in the saloon, just the usual drunks and miners looking for a watering hole or a poke at one of the girls in the establishment across the way. I didn't mind it none, some peace and quiet would do me good, along with some spirits.

Billy returned with a bottle of cheap whiskey and a grimy glass that had seen better days. I reached for the bottle and pain shot up my side, causing a grunt to escape my lips. I wasn't a medicine man, but I was pretty sure I was dying. I told that idiot with the scattergun to keep it trained on the passengers, but he was a curious sort, and I got winged because of his lack of focus. Could have been worse I suppose, 'cause he got dead.

Someone was tickling the ivories on Billy's old piano, filling the room with a tune. It was a soft melody, but it scratched the back of my mind as if I'd heard it before. I couldn't quite place it and gave up trying.

The whiskey burned as it slid down my throat, it was a good burn. Two more followed suit and then I gave it a rest, hoping it would take the edge off the lead stuck in my chest. My pa used to tell me, "hope in one hand and shit in the other and see which would fill up faster." He was a smart man and I was a stubborn fool.

The music stopped and the man who had been playing sauntered over to my table. A blood-red bandana was wrapped around his head, keeping a heap of wheat-colored hair at bay. I kept one hand on my pistol just under the table in case he wanted to try and put the final nail in the coffin.

"Leave me be, stranger."

He flashed me a smile colder than a January morning in the high mountains. Could have been the blood loss, but I swear something flashed behind his eyes, just a flicker of movement beneath the surface as if his face were a mask.

"You've been a naughty boy, Jack."

The stranger's voice slithered through the air, a cat on the prowl looking for some unsuspecting prey. It made my skin want to crawl off my bones and hide in a dark corner.

"Is that so? And what makes you think you know a damn thing about me?"

I pulled the hammer back on my pistol, trying to move it slow enough not to make a noise, but when it clicked into place, firing it would have been the only thing louder.

The strange man smiled a crooked smile and took a seat in one of the empty chairs. He drummed his fingers on the table, his long and pointed fingernails leaving small scratches in the old wood.

"What do you want?"

The question caused a coughing fit to rise in my chest, sending waves of pain rolling through my body. Something wet was making its way up my throat and I put a hand in front of my mouth to stop it from flying out. The bloody phlegm I hocked up was a bad sign.

"I want you, Jack. You're dying and I've come to collect."

I returned the smile and pulled the trigger on my pistol. I was expecting to gut shot the stranger sitting in front of me, what I wasn't expecting was a misfire. The man smiled even wider and sat back in his chair. I jerked the gun up above the table and pulled the trigger three more times, each one produced nothing but a dull click.

"Who are you?"

"I go by many names, but you can call me Sam."

"Sam, you old goat, how do you know we don't want him?" A new voice boomed from the bar, shaking the walls of the saloon and spilling dust from the rafters. Sam sneered. He refused to look back at the speaker, instead poured himself a drink from my bottle of whiskey.

The man walked over from the bar, taking a seat next to Sam. He was an older gentleman with a long beard that had seen better days and eyes grayer than granite. Like Sam, something seemed to move behind those eyes, something old.

"And who the hell are you and what do you want?' I asked, taking my drink back from Sam which elicited a sneer from the man.

"I'm nobody really, but you can call me Pete, and I'm here to save you from damnation."

The old timer didn't look the part of one of those sin-busters thumping on their good books and preaching about salvation, but who was I to judge? There was a familiarity to the old man as if I'd known him for a long time. There was also an overwhelming sense of disappointment rolling off him.

"Jack, he's right," Pete said, pointing to Sam. "You have sinned. Right now, your fate could go either way. Up or down."

"Nah, he's damned and he knows it. Too many sins to count if you ask me."

Sam was grinning again, this time there was a bit of warmth coming off his smile. It wasn't a pleasant kind of warmth either.

"Get the hell out of here and leave me be. Let me get soaked in peace!"

I unloaded the dud bullets from my pistol and was about to reload when the saloon went completely dark, save for a small circle of orange light above the table. All the sounds of breathing, shuffling glasses, and murmurs ceased to exist, leaving nothing but silence to echo throughout the room. Sam and the old man stared at me, not speaking.

"What is this?"

"It's your death, Jack. You'll be dead in less than hour. The bullet clipped something important in that poor excuse of a body you have and you're bleeding out. I'm sorry," Pete said.

"Yep, you'll be belly up in the boot hill before morning," Sam said with a chuckle.

I believed them. The slow trickle of blood and the sinking feeling in my guts verified it. I finished off the bottle of whiskey, happy that the pain in my chest had finally dulled.

"Well, isn't that swell? So what happens now?"

"We figure out where you're going to go. You're coming with one of us."

"More than likely you're coming with me. I've got a lot of fun things planned, Jack. Things you'll enjoy," Sam said.

The orange light above the table flared at the end of Sam's sentence and set ghost lights dancing in front of my eyes for a moment. The smell of rotten eggs smacked my face and I almost lost all the wonderful whiskey I'd drank.

"That's enough," Pete said.

At his command, the orange light softened until it was replaced by a glowing blue orb. The pain my chest faded which was nice, as well as the buzz of the whiskey which wasn't nice.

"The problem is that you've tip-toed the line, Jack. It could really go either way," Sam said. "Which brings us to the here and now."

Sam drummed his fingers on the table again, his face locked in that fake grin that fit him like a tailored suit.

I didn't like where this was going, I needed to stall, buy some time. That's when it hit me.

"Well, I tell you what, how about we play a few hands before I go?" I asked. "Doesn't seem like either of you are in a rush."

Sam scratched his chin, then clasped his hands together.

"Why the hell not?" Sam said.

"It will only delay the inevitable, Jack," Pete said.

"I've played cards here hundreds of times, it would be nice to play another round before I go."

"Very well."

A deck of cards appeared on the table from out of nowhere. There wasn't a poof or a pop, they simply were there when moments before they were not. I picked them up and they were familiar as if I had played with them for years.

The cards shuffled as natural as a waterfall and slicker than hot grease on a fry pan. I cut the deck with one hand and shuffled them again with a smile creeping into the corner of my lips.

"Okay boys, here it is: five card draw, let's play a few."

Sam scooted his chair up closer to the table. "We need some music."

He snapped his fingers causing a spark to flash as if he'd just hit steel against flint. Somewhere in the darkness, a fiddle started to play, the music was chaotic, manic and rushed, but buried deep within the discord was something catchy.

Pete sighed and scooted up to the table as well. He snapped his fingers and Sam's fiddle playing stopped, replaced by a typical piano tune. He nodded toward the cards, his eyes warm and kind.

I played the first hand watching. Observing. The old timer didn't move a muscle in his face the entire time. No twitch, no smile, hell, not even a frown. Just a deadpan glare at the cards in front him, as if he were sleeping. I'd almost given up hope that I'd be able to read him when the corner of his eye shifted. There it was.

He won that hand, eliciting a round of cursing from Sam. Many of the words I was intimately familiar with, others, well I couldn't even tell what language they were in. I may have lost the round, but I'd gained some potentially priceless knowledge.

The next round, Sam won. He had so many tells that it was hard to pick which one was authentic and which one was bullshit. He was going to be a bigger challenge.

We played probably a dozen hands. The whole time I watched the two men. Verifying tells and forcing situations on the other two. It was hard to focus, given that I was supposed to be dying and going to heaven or hell, but I tried.

I shuffled the deck a few times, the cards now an extension of my hands. After the right amount, I moved the deck toward Pete.

"What's wrong? I'm not good enough to cut the deck?" Sam asked, placing his hand across his chest and casting a frown that belonged on a stage my way.

"I don't trust you."

"Moi?"

Pete tapped the top of the deck and pushed them back my way. Bold move. His mistake.

I smiled and dealt the cards out. The entire time, Sam drummed his fingers, louder and louder, never breaking eye contact with me.

"You know, you're already dead. You've bled out and you're lying face down on that grimy table in good old, Billy Brock's saloon."

Trying not to listen to Sam was like trying not to breathe, as each moment thundered on, it was harder and harder to endure.

"Face down, blood pooling at your boots. Hell, you might have already shit your pants by now. You've seen enough dead bodies to know that happens."

I hesitated dealing the last round of cards. I put the deck down and rubbed my temples.

"Before we end this, can I get a drink?" I asked.

"Sure thing, Jack. For you, anything."

Sam snapped his fingers, causing the sparks to fly through the air once again. This time though, a puff of smoke appeared over the table. When the smoke cleared, a bottle of whiskey sat in its place. He poured me a shot and placed it in front of me.

To say I'd drank a lot in my years would be like saying it was cold in the Dakota Territory, both true, but understatements. It didn't just get cold in the Dakota Territory, it got colder than a witch's tit in a snowstorm cold. Needless to say, I knew my whiskeys, which was why I was surprised when I drank what was in my glass. I'd never, in any of my outlawin' years, tasted a whiskey like that. It burned hotter than a midsummer's day in Texas, searing my throat the whole way down. Yet it was good. There was a smokiness to it that I'd never tasted before mixed with a spice that had my tongue begging for more. It reminded me of the time I'd bedded that little Mexican rose near the border. She was wild, full of life, and full of sin.

"What in the hell is that?"

"Not many have had my own special cask. Consider yourself lucky."

"Bah, devil piss and nothing else," Pete said. He poured a shot from a silver flask he had stashed away in his coat pocket. "Try this."

I sipped it, unsure of what to expect. Instead of a burn, it was mellow, smooth, and complex. It was the moment before the sun rose above the mountains, that quiet time that you know you should get moving, but you can't because you're lost in all those colors marching through the sky.

"Devil piss? It's better than that fluffy juice you call a drink."

My stomach was happy again, warm and radiant. While they were bickering about whose whiskey was better, I picked up the deck and dealt the last round of cards, sliding a card off the bottom when I came to my pile.

I watched as they picked up their cards, looking for the tells I had identified. Satisfied with what they were showing me, I felt confident with my next move.

"How about we make this interesting?" I said.

"You mean playing cards with me isn't interesting enough?" Sam asked.

"What exactly are you getting at?" Pete asked.

"If smiley here wins, then I guess I'm going to the lake of fire, and if you win, then you can take me to the great range in the sky."

"And if you win?" the old timer asked.

"Glad you asked…if I win, then you leave me be and let me get on my own way. Neither of you takes me anywhere."

Pete arched one of his eyebrows while Sam laughed and slapped his knee.

"Now you're playing with fire, I love it!" Sam said.

"You would gamble your eternal soul?" Pete asked.

"Better than you two bastards deciding for me."

"Done! But we're playing stud this time. Let Fate decide what's going to happen," Sam said, slapping the table. The floor shook from the blow and rattled my teeth.

"Are you sure?" The old timer asked, his eyes heavy with concern.

"Yes, indeed. Let's do this."

"Okay, Jack. You are free to make your own choices. Done."

The room vibrated again. It wasn't as strong as when Sam had slapped the table, but it was no less noticeable.

I grabbed my cards. Two Aces, two Eights, and a King to round it all out. I did my best to hide my disappointment. It wasn't a bad hand, but I was hoping for something more. My soul was on the line. Something had gone wrong. Perhaps I had missed a card in the shuffle, or maybe I counted wrong.

Pete gave me a heavy look, his eyes full of sorrow. With a small shake of his head, he put his cards on the table.

"Fold."

I raised an eyebrow, keeping all other emotion off my face. Then I turned my attention back to Sam. Pete's gaze bore through me like a Bowie knife, cutting through my soul. I tried my best to push it out of my mind.

"Really? You're going to fold? You know we aren't upping the ante at all. You could just play and see how the cards drop," Sam said with a half sneer.

"I've lost," was all Pete said.

"How about you, what have you got?" I asked.

Sam placed his cards on the table, splayed out in a perfect fan. He sat back in his chair, placing his hands behind his head.

"You know what, Jack? I like you. I feel like if circumstances were different, we could be friends."

His ear twitched, and he blinked his eyes fast three times in succession. These were different tells I hadn't seen before. What was his game?

"Not sure things would work out too well between the two of us," I said.

"Perhaps. However, that doesn't change the fact that you and I are cut from the same block. That's why I'm willing to strike a deal."

"I haven't heard too many good things about your deals. Never end well."

My chest started to throb. Dull at first, like a burr caught my shirt and rubbing the wrong way. Yet, it didn't take long before the pain increased and it got hard to breathe. I winced placing my hand on my side, it came away bloody.

"See, you ain't got long. You're going to pass soon and from the looks of it, you're coming with me."

"What about our arrangement?"

"Let me get to that."

"Sam, no altering the deal, just play the game," Pete said, balling his hand into a fist.

"This doesn't concern you, old man. This is between Jack and me. He started this carousel a spinnin'. Besides, you've lost already, you've folded, so shut your yap."

The old timer frowned but stayed quiet. I tried to study Sam's face for something familiar, anything that would give me an edge as to what he was playing at, but each time I tried, the pain should lance through my body causing a coughing fit.

"Let's forget this game, call it a draw. I'll give you another ten years, and let me tell you, son, they'll be the best years you'll ever have. You want money? Done. You want women? Done. You'll live a life of luxury."

"What's the catch?" I asked, wiping the blood from my mouth with a dirty handkerchief.

"Do I have to spell it out for you? You come live with me when it's over, Jack."

His fingers drummed so loud on the table it hurt my ears. I glanced at my cards again. Aces and Eights, King high. The options weighed on me, on one hand, I could live out a few more years and then be damned to hell. On the other, if my intuition was right, I could win this game and walk away free.

"I don't think so, show me what you got," I said, laying my cards out on the table.

The smile disappeared from Sam's face, replaced with a sneer. The drumming stopped and he balled his hand into a fist, ripping up pieces of the table with his nails.

Sam flipped his cards over, he had a 10, Jack, Queen, and King. He held onto his last card for a moment before revealing it. It was another Jack.

I smiled and clapped my hands together which brought about another wave of pain. I coughed up a wad of bloody phlegm onto the table and almost fell out of my chair; however, I was able to choke out a couple words.

"I win."

"No, Jack. You lose," Pete said.

"I tried to help, but you wanted to play your game. Cheaters never prosper, Jack." Sam said.

My vision blurred to the point that Sam and Pete were nothing but fuzzy shapes, yet somehow Sam's rictus grin was still clear.

"We had a deal," I said, though my voice came through as a raspy whisper.

"Indeed we did, and we'll honor your deal," Pete said. "We won't be taking you anywhere and we'll let you be."

I forced a smile onto my face, and even that small act brought about a spasm of pain in my guts.

Mustering all the determination I could, I sat back into my chair.

"Fix me up," I said.

Sam made a tsk-tsk sound and shook his head.

"I'm afraid not. Gonna let you be."

My heart dropped into my stomach. "But the deal!"

"Deal was we wouldn't take you anywhere, nothing in there about making you whole again. Wording, Jack, it's all about the wording," Sam said.

"Sorry, Jack. But you brought this upon yourself. I'm afraid I can't intervene. Goodbye." With those words, Pete disappeared.

"I may be a lot of things, but I follow rules and agreements. So long," Sam said.

The sound of the saloon returned with Sam's disappearance. It happened so quick that it took me off guard for a moment, sending me spinning. However, the sounds were muffled, as if I was on one end of a tunnel and everyone else was on the other.

The pain in my chest was muffled as well, dull. It was still there, but only annoying instead of debilitating.

Somehow, I'd fallen onto the floor. I don't remember dropping, just one minute I was sitting at the table, the next I was on the ground staring at a pool of blood that must have been mine. People were rushing toward me, but I couldn't hear anything anymore other than the sound of my own breathing, which was getting shorter and shallower by the second.

Things went dark again and for a horrible second, I thought I'd gone blind. I felt around, hoping to feel the dust-covered floorboards, there was nothing but cool air. At least there was that. Things had gotten so damned hot as of late.

When my eyesight returned, I was back to sitting at the table. There was a mass of folks right next to me crowding around something. I scooted out of the chair to give them some space which is when I noticed what they were crowding around.

My dead body was on the ground. The people weren't crowding around me to help neither, they were picking me clean, grabbing my gun, boots, and my nice pocket watch that was a gift from my pa.

"Bunch of vultures, aren't they, Jack?" Sam said from behind me.

"What the hell?"

"Indeed."

"I'm dead!" I think I wanted to say it as a question, but it came out of my mouth as a statement as I watched the mob take everything of value of my corpse.

"Yes you are, which brings me to why I'm here," Sam said.

He walked over to my side and looked at my body. He made a tsking sound and then turned to me.

"You came back to drag me to hell?"

"I wish it were that simple, but we had a deal you see. I can't take you, neither can Heaven it seems, not that they'd want you."

"Then what what's going to happen to me?"

The saloon vanished under a blanket of darkness so thick I didn't think I would even be able to move through it. I'd seen darkness before, spending my fair share of starless nights out in the wilds, but this was something else in entirely.

"Seems like you're going to spend the rest of your existence in Purgatory, Jack. Not a fun place."

The darkness wasn't quiet. Things moved all around me, getting closer every second. Worse than that, the things spoke. I tried to cover my ears, but it only made them speak louder. The voices of dead friends and relatives. My grandpappy telling me that I was a worthless runt that should have died years ago. My mother screaming in agony as my pa buried an ax in her spine. Other things spoke as well. Ancient things that wanted to be free from the darkness as much as I did.

There was as snap of fingers followed by a brilliant flash of orange light. It soon dimmed, casting just enough light I could see the ground below my feet. It was covered in wet, decaying leaves that tended to move ever so often as if something was just beneath the surface.

The light came from a piece of coal smoldering in Sam's hand. He no longer smiled at me, instead wore a slight frown. Sam let out a sigh and tossed me the piece of coal. I reached out instinctively and caught it. I almost dropped it to the ground, halfway expecting it to burn me, but it didn't. Not at first anyway. The longer I held onto it, the warmer it got. It didn't take long before I had to transfer it from hand to hand.

"No, Jack. You see, I really do like you. It takes guts to hustle the devil. That's why I'm leaving you with that gift. Don't lose it, because I don't think you want to be out here in the dark all lonesome and such."

With that, he was gone.

I bounced the burning coal in my hand as I walked. I walked for hours with nothing but the maddening noises of the dark to keep me company. I tried to use my coat to carry the stone, but it muffled the soft light and the things got too close for comfort.

As I continued along, I came to a pumpkin patch which was the first different thing I'd seen since arriving. With nothing else to do, I pulled out my knife and started carving one of the pumpkins. It would make an excellent lantern in which to carry the glowing coal. Something to light my way.